He Said He Had Waited Too Long To Hold Her.

She put her hand in his but as he drew her closer, she protested nervously, "I've never danced with a man before. I don't know what to do."

"It's like walking. Shift your weight back and forth between your feet, and let me give you your direction."

Shakira felt enclosed and safe. The music seemed to flow through them, wrap around them, binding them together, so that after a time it seemed as though something else created the dance, using their bodies.

A singing heat tingled on her skin when he touched her. His hand moved against her bare back, and she felt a shivering response down her spine. He bent his head to murmur something, and even his breath against her neck caused a delicious melting.

Then he dropped his hands and she knew she had been wrong about the bonds that linked them. They were not the product of the music, but something else. Because they were still there, binding her to him, when the music stopped. And she regretted that this moment ever had to end.

Dear Reader,

Silhouette Desire is starting the New Year off with a bang as we introduce our brand-new family-centric continuity, DYNASTIES: THE ASHTONS. Set in the lush wine-making country of Napa Valley, California, the Ashtons are a family divided by a less-than-fatherly patriarch. We think you'll be thoroughly entranced by all the drama and romance when the wonderful Eileen Wilks starts things off with *Entangled*. Look for a new book in the series each month…all year long.

The New Year also brings new things from the fabulous Dixie Browning as she launches DIVAS WHO DISH. You'll love her sassy heroine in *Her Passionate Plan B*. SONS OF THE DESERT, Alexandra Sellers's memorable series, is back this month with the dramatic conclusion, *The Fierce and Tender Sheikh*. RITA® Award-winning author Cindy Gerard will thrill you with the heart-stopping hero in *Between Midnight and Morning*. (My favorite time of the night. What about you?)

Rounding out the month are two clever stories about shocking romances: Shawna Delacorte's tale of a sexy hero who falls for his best friend's sister, *In Forbidden Territory,* and Shirley Rogers's story of a secretary who ends up winning her boss in a bachelor auction, *Business Affairs*.

Here's to a New Year's resolution we should all keep: indulging in more *desire!*

Happy reading,

Melissa Jeglinski

Melissa Jeglinski
Senior Editor, Silhouette Desire

Please address questions and book requests to:
Silhouette Reader Service
U.S.: 3010 Walden Ave., P.O. Box 1325, Buffalo, NY 14269
Canadian: P.O. Box 609, Fort Erie, Ont. L2A 5X3

THE FIERCE AND TENDER SHEIKH

ALEXANDRA SELLERS

Published by Silhouette Books
America's Publisher of Contemporary Romance

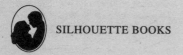 **SILHOUETTE BOOKS**

ISBN 0-373-76629-7

THE FIERCE AND TENDER SHEIKH

Copyright © 2005 by Alexandra Sellers.

The author would like to express her grateful thanks to Amina Shah and the publisher for permission to use the story of Yunus and the Well of Sweetness. It has been retold from ARABIAN FAIRY TALES by Amina Shah (Octagon Press Ltd., London 1989).

ALEXANDRA SELLERS

is the author of over twenty-five novels and a feline language text published in 1997 and still selling.

Born and raised in Canada, Alexandra first came to London as a drama student. Now she lives near Hampstead Heath with her husband, Nick. They share housekeeping with Monsieur, who jumped through the window one day and announced, as cats do, that he was moving in.

What she would miss most on a desert island is shared laughter.

Readers can write to Alexandra at P.O. Box 9449, London NW3 2WH, UK, England.

1
Hani

Hani's Dream

In the dream she had a name. Her own true name. In the dream she knew who she was.

She wasn't alone, in the dream. She had a home and a family, her own true family. The beloved faces she had lost so long ago were restored to her, in other faces that somehow belonged to her.

She wasn't hungry, in the dream, and they told her that she would never go hungry again. And there was water there, clean water, to wash in as well as to drink. Nor did she sleep in mud under a filthy tent, nor in a tiny, stifling room with bars on the windows. No, she had a bed so large and comfortable and clean she could not sleep for the freshness and wonder of it, and a room so airy and beautiful that in the dream she wept to see it.

In the dream they said—her family—that it belonged to her by right and that she would never again be lost to them. People called her Princess in the dream, as if she were someone to cherish. Someone important, someone worth loving.

In the dream, she was a woman.

One

The desert lay smoking under the burning sun, rugged and inhospitable all the way to the distant mountains. Cutting across it, the highway made no compromise with the terrain, a grey, featureless ribbon streaking over gully and flat with ruthless self-importance: the hostile conspiring with the inflexible to produce a faceless indifference to human need.

A large flatbed truck, its load covered with a bright blue plastic tarpaulin and fixed with ropes, was roaring over the lonely stretch of highway, smoky dust rising from its passing, as if the flat tarmac were setting fire to its wheels and it had to keep moving or be consumed.

Far behind, on the otherwise empty road, in a glinting silver car that was quickly gaining on the truck, Sheikh Sharif Azad al Dauleh flicked his eyes from the map flattened against the steering wheel to the view out the window. No sign of his destination yet. All that met his gaze was the barren landscape, sere and rust-coloured, scratched with gullies as if by a giant claw, dotted with parched scrub. As barren as any Bagestani desert, and yet unmistakably alien. He could not feel at home here.

It was a printed map, on which the site he was searching the desert for was marked only in pen. *Burry Hill Detention Centre* had been scratched above a rough *X* near the line that was the road, some miles from the nearest town. His eyes flicked over the landscape, looking for evidence of a side road. According to his information, it would not be signposted. The general public was not encouraged to drop in at refugee camps.

He tossed the map down and sighed. A difficult mission, the Sultan had said. But neither Ashraf nor he himself had had any idea of the nature of the difficulties that would confront him. The assignment to find a lost member of the royal family, somewhere in the world's refugee camps, was not merely a logistical nightmare; it was an emotional black hole. The scale of suffering he had seen was something no one could be prepared for.

The truck was belching a noxious, thick grey smoke. The sheikh put his foot down harder and pulled into the passing lane.

At the back of the truck, behind the veil of smoke and fumes, a bundle wrapped in dust-coloured cloth flapped wildly, as if about to be torn from its mountings: a boy, clinging to the ropes. The truck had a stowaway.

A thin, starved stowaway, agile as a monkey, who was coming down off the top of the load with an audacity that made Sharif's groin contract. He watched as the boy stretched down one thin leg till his bare foot found the bumper. Then, standing, he glanced over his shoulder to check the road behind. Sharif realized with horror that his own car must be in the boy's blind spot, for he now leaned out at the side of the truck opposite to the car, clinging with one hand, as if preparing to jump.

Sharif cursed in impotent amazement. Was he watching a suicide? But even as he slapped his hand to the horn, the stowaway lifted an arm and tossed something under the truck's wheels.

The sound of an explosion drowned his own blaring horn. Ahead, the truck slewed into his path and shuddered to a halt. Pulling his own wheel to avoid a collision, he saw the small, slim figure leap nimbly down into the road directly in front of him.

Only then did the boy discover his presence. He flung a look of stunned horror towards the oncoming car, his eyes locking with Sharif's for one appalling second, landed awkwardly, grimaced with pain, and rolled in a desperate attempt to get out of his path.

The car's tires bit hard into the super-hot tarmac, screaming and jolting in protest as Sharif simultaneously hauled on the emergency brake and dragged at the wheel. Gravel flailed up against the body and windows with a sound like gunfire, and the hot, sharp smell of rubber pierced the air.

The silver car came to rest on the shoulder, its nose a foot or two from the banked edge that slanted sharply down to the desert floor. Ahead, the truck was angled the other way, its body forming a wide V with the car. Between them lay the boy, his thin arms wrapping his head, panting hard. Around him was a spread of fallen objects—chocolate bars, a toy, something that glittered pathetically in the harsh sun. An orange, its bright colour shocking in this dun-coloured landscape, rolled lazily along the tarmac.

The silence of settling dust. Sharif opened his door and got out. He was tall, as tall as the Sultan himself, with a warrior's build and a proud, some might say arrogant, posture. His long face was marked by a square jaw and a straight nose inherited from his foreign mother. His upper lip was well-formed, his firm, full lower lip the sign of a deep and passionate nature which few ever saw. Dark eyes under low-set, almost straight brows showed the intense intelligence of the mind behind. His cheekbones were strong, his skin smooth. His fine black hair was cut short and neat, the curl tamed back from the wide, clear forehead.

The boy sat up, fighting to catch his breath. He seemed otherwise unhurt.

"You little fool," Sharif said.

"Where…where did you…come from?" the boy panted.

His thick, sunburnt hair was chopped ragged. In the sharply revealed bone structure of the starved little face, the jaw was square but delicate for a boy, sloping down to a pointed chin. His wide, full mouth was too big for his thin face. So were the eyes. He was too young for the age in his eyes—but so were they all, in the camps. Sharif guessed him at about fourteen.

Sharif gave a bark of angry laughter. "Where did *I* come from? What the hell were you doing? You're lucky to be alive!"

For a moment the boy simply gazed at him wide-eyed, taking in the sight of Sharif's proud, stern handsomeness, the flowing white djellaba and keffiyeh so alien to this land.

"Yes. Thank you," said the boy.

This was so unexpected that this time Sharif's laughter was genuine. He drew a gold case out of the pocket of his djellaba, extracted a thin black cigar, and set it between his teeth. The boy, meanwhile, still breathing hard, got up on his knees and reached for a chocolate bar, then grimaced with sudden pain and turned to nurse one ankle.

Sharif paused in the act of pulling out his lighter. "Are you hurt?"

"No," the boy lied, as if to admit to any weakness would be dangerous. Setting his teeth against pain, he turned doggedly to the task of gathering up his loot.

Sharif set his foot on a blue plastic ring in a brightly printed cardboard mount just as the boy's fingers reached for it. The boy looked up into the dark eyes so far above, his gaze challenging, assessing.

"How bad?" Sharif asked.

The boy shrugged.

"How badly are you hurt?" Sharif insisted.

"What do you care? Does it make you feel better to think that you're concerned? When you go on your way in your nice shiny car will it give you a warm feeling to know that you asked after my health?"

The cynicism was brutal, for it told of years of suffering, and the boy was still only a child. That such complete absence of trust could exist in a human breast suddenly struck Sharif as deeply tragic. He suddenly, urgently wanted this damaged child to understand that there was genuine goodness in the world.

Simultaneously he derided himself for the sentiment. He had visited nothing but scenes from hell for weeks past, and he had managed to keep his head above water. Why now? Why this skinny kid who trusted no one? He emphatically did not want to be drawn in. It was a one-way trip. Take one member of suffering humanity personally and there was no end to it. Like a surgeon, he had to keep a clinical distance.

"Don't be a fool. Get in the car. I'll take you to a doctor."

The boy visibly flinched. "No, thanks. Are you going to lift your foot? I need this." He tried to pull whatever it was out from under Sharif's foot, but succeeded only in tearing the packaging.

They had both forgotten the trucker. Having moved his truck off the road, he now came towards them at a furious jog.

"You bloody little scum!" he cried, descending on the boy. "What were you playing at? You're one of those bloody refugees, aren't you?"

He grabbed the boy's wrist and dragged him to his feet, spilling all his gathered possessions onto the ground again. The boy cried out with pain.

"Refugees?" Sharif Azad al Dauleh queried softly, his voice cutting through the other's anger.

There was a pause as the trucker absorbed the powerful

frame, the proud posture, the clothing from that other desert a world away.

"That's Burry Hill over there." He nodded towards the cruel, uncompromising rows of curling razor wire just visible in the distance across the bleak scrubland, ignoring the boy silently struggling in his ruthless hold. "It's not as secure as the others. People say they can get out, but there's nowhere to go, so they have to go back. I've heard of this trick—they throw some kind of firework under your wheels and when you stop they jump off and are out over the desert before you can catch them.

"But not this time, eh?" He jerked at the boy's wrist and showed his teeth. "Not this time."

"Let me go, you stinking camel-stuffer!" shrieked the boy, suddenly abandoning English to revert to a *patois* that seemed to be a mixture of languages, of which Bagestani Arabic and Parvani formed the chief part. A stream of insult followed.

Sharif flicked the gold lighter alive, a smile twitching his lips for the rich fluency of the invective as the boy informed the trucker that he was a man who didn't know one end of a goat from the other, but wasn't particular about it anyway. He briefly bent to the flame. When he lifted his head again his eyes fell on the boy's contorted face, and for a moment he went perfectly still.

"Come here, you little—" The trucker was trying to deliver a kick, but even with his hurt foot, the boy was proving too agile. Beside the well-fed driver, he looked like a stick insect.

"Eater of the vomit of dogs!"

The lighter closed with an expensive click and Sharif Azad al Dauleh lifted his head and took the cigar out of his mouth.

"Let him go."

At the sound of the cold command, the trucker's eyes popped in disbelief. "What?" he demanded.

"You're bigger than he is. And you can remember your last meal."

"What's that got to do with it? He could have killed us both! He's a thief, too! Look at all this stuff—nicked, for sure!" cried the driver, indicating the litter of items on the ground.

"Let him go."

"You're out…"

Looking up into the taller man's eyes, the driver hesitated. Arms crossed over his chest, eyes narrowed against the smoke, Sharif smiled. The boy, taking advantage of a slackened grip, broke free and limped past Sharif to shelter, panting, behind the open car door.

"I think you're mistaken. You ran over a plastic bottle," Sharif said.

There was a long moment of challenge. The trucker looked from the dark-eyed sheikh to the dark-eyed boy, and sneered.

"I get it. One of your own, is he?"

"Yes," said Sharif softly. "One of my own."

Something in his face made the other man step back. "Well, I don't have time for this," he blustered. "I've got a timetable!" He spat violently down at the boy's strewn possessions, then turned and strode back towards his own vehicle.

A moment later the truck was roaring down the road again, as though trying to escape the smoke of its own exhaust.

Sharif Azad al Dauleh remained where he was for a moment, gazing out over the desert towards the barbed wire and the painful glitter of the metal roofs, trying to make sense of what he thought he'd seen. Maybe he'd had too much sun.

"Come out!" he ordered, without raising his voice.

He turned his head as the slim figure straightened from behind the door.

The boy looked starved. The bare arms under the baggy T-shirt sleeves were painfully thin, and the long neck and hollow cheeks only intensified the impression that he needed a square meal. But there was no mistaking the resemblance, once he had seen it.

"What's your name?" Sharif asked softly, in Bagestani Arabic.

The boy looked at him, breathing hard, a wounded animal only waiting for the return of his strength to flee. At the question, his eyes went blank.

"I have a reason for asking," Sharif prodded in an urgent voice.

In the same pithy language he had used with the trucker, the boy advised him on the precise placement of his reason and his question. The advice was colourful and inventive.

"Tell me your father's name."

For one unguarded moment, the boy's face became a mask of grief. Then his eyes went blank again, and he shrugged in a *to hell with you* kind of way and limped painfully to pick up an orange. Sharif lifted his foot to free whatever the toy was, and for a moment the boy gave off a deep animal wariness, as if this might be a prelude to violence. He didn't rank Sharif an inch higher than he did the trucker.

One eyebrow raised in dry comment on the boy's suspicions, Sharif bent and picked up the object. The boy stowed the rest of the things in his pockets under the loose T-shirt, then stood a few feet from Sharif.

"It's mine. Give it to me."

Sharif took the cigar from his mouth. "Didn't you steal it?"

"What do you care? I stole it, you didn't. It's mine. If you keep it, you're a thief, too, no better than me. Give it to me."

The boy was favouring his foot so carefully Sharif guessed the dance with the trucker had broken a bone. The important thing was to get him to a doctor. He would worry about the other later.

He tossed the object to the boy and jerked his head. "Get in the car."

But the boy snatched it from the air, whirled and, not limping nearly so heavily now, made for the embankment.

"Don't be a fool!" Sharif snapped. "You're hurt! Let me take you to a doctor!"

His mouth stretched in a mocking smile, the boy flicked a backward glance. And with sunlight and shadow just so, his cheekbones and eyes again revealed that shape the Cup Companion knew so well.

"What's your name? Who is your family?"

But the boy slithered down the slope and was running almost before he landed on the desert floor. A moment later, deft as an Aboriginal hunter, he had disappeared into the landscape.

Two

"**I**s it you, my son? Did God bring you luck?"

Farida lay on the bed beside her baby, her sweat-damped dark hair loosely knotted in a scarf, trying to comfort the whimpering infant with a sugar-soaked knot of cloth. As Hani entered, the young mother looked up, wiping a hand over her wet face with a sigh. The room was at cooking temperature, though the only natural light came from a small barred window that was too high to see out.

The boy approached and began to draw things out from under his T-shirt. Chocolate bars, a bracelet, a child's teething ring, oranges appeared in quick succession on the bed in front of Farida. The tired young mother smiled and reached out to turn the items over, one by one.

"How do you do it?" she asked, shaking her head in admiration.

The boy only shrugged and set down a few more items—some useful in themselves, some that would be traded. It was a foolish question: Hani managed things no one else dreamed of.

He was a born forager. Perhaps it was the elfin quickness, or simply long experience and luck, but Hani kept his family supplied while others went without. It had been a happy day for Farida when the boy had attached himself to her, for although he was young and slight, he had spent years in the camps, and he was tough, with the intelligence of a much older man. His speed and cunning often protected them where a grown man would have used brawn.

Probably he used his fluent English to fool the people in the shops. No one in the camp knew of his talent—and how useful that was! Hani always knew what was going on in the camp, simply by eavesdropping around the administrative office. It was he who had first heard the news of the Sultan's emissary.

The boy brought one last item out of a pocket and dropped it on the bed. A black leather wallet.

Farida's mouth formed an O as she saw it: Hani didn't often pick pockets. The wallet was obviously expensive, made of fine, soft leather. Farida reached for it, and her fingers found the cash inside with a little sigh. Quickly she counted it, and smiled. Oh, how easy such an amount would make their lives, for days, weeks!

She passed the money to Hani, who reached for the plastic yogurt container, stuffed with a rusty pot scratcher, a bar of green soap and a sponge, that sat on the little stand between a dishwashing bowl and a bucket of water. He lifted out the inner pot and tucked the money inside the larger pot, then carefully restored the inner container and set the pot down again. Their bank.

"Barakullah! What is this?" Farida hissed. She stared down at the gold seal and the delicate calligraphy of the business card she had found in the wallet. "'His Excellency Sharif Azad al Dauleh…'" As she understood, her mouth fell open in an almost comical expression of mingled astonishment and dismay. *"You have robbed a Bagestani diplomat?"* she cried

in a hoarse whisper, for the walls were not thick. "How? Where was he? How did you get close to him?"

Hani scooped a dipperful of water from the bucket to rinse the blue teething ring over the bowl, then splashed his face and neck with small, bony hands. He handed the rubber ring to the baby.

"On the road. His car was behind the truck I hitched a ride on. He might have killed me, but his reflexes were very fast."

Farida stared. "Were you hurt?"

The boy shrugged.

"Tell me what happened."

Farida got to her feet and began to pace the tiny area of free space in the centre of the cramped room as she listened to the boy's recital. Over her shoulder the baby chewed the teething ring and watched Hani, wide-eyed and curious.

"My son, he saved your life, and he saved you from a beating, and you stole his wallet?" she said, when he had finished.

Hani only looked at her.

"Oh, Hani, but think!—it must be *him!* Sultan Ashraf's envoy!"

For days the detention centre had been buzzing with the rumour that a high official from Bagestan was expected at the camp. His reason for coming wasn't known, but hopes were very high among the Bagestanis in the camp that it had something to do with repatriating them, now that the new Sultan was safe on the throne. And even the ragtag representatives of the half-dozen other strife-torn nations here were half convinced it meant their own salvation.

"He was travelling alone, not even a driver. Diplomats on missions to refugee camps don't come without assistants and the media," the boy said with cynical wisdom.

"Perhaps his entourage is coming later. Why else would such a man be in a place like this? *Ya Allah!* The Sultan's own Cup Companion! If only he doesn't realize you are the thief, Hani! Do you think he will recognize you if he sees you again?"

An abrupt knocking sounded against the door.

The young mother jerked spasmodically, clutching the wallet, and the baby opened her mouth, let the new teething ring fall, and began to wail again.

"What shall we do?" Farida hissed.

"Give it to me," Hani said and, stretching out one thin arm, plucked the wallet from Farida's trembling hand. In a moment it had disappeared again under the baggy T-shirt.

"Hani!" Farida whispered, but another knock sounded, and there was no time to argue. Her eyes black with anxiety, Farida opened the door.

It was one of the "guards," men from the refugee community who were badged and assigned the task of liaison between the staff and inhabitants of the community. What the camp authorities didn't understand, or didn't want to, was that on those badges a ruthless camp mafia was founded and nourished.

He frowned at Hani.

"You went into town today," he growled in the camp *patois*. His eyes went past Farida to the bed, where the pathetic rewards of the foraging expedition still lay. "Let me see!"

Hani leapt for him, grabbing his arm, in a bid to protect the hard-won treasures. But the guard was big and ruthless, and merely threw the boy to one side, so that he fell against the sink. For a moment he clung there, half kneeling, nursing his injured ankle.

He cursed the guard with the fierce contempt of the powerless. "A baby soother!" he said. "Do you want to suck on it? Maybe your rotten teeth will grow again!"

Then he was up again, jumping onto the brute's back as he bent over the bed. His small fist pummelled the man's ear. A big, powerful hand grabbed the thin wrist and brutally twisted, so that the boy cried out and submitted. He was tossed down like a sack of waste.

The guard's eye had fallen on the telltale sparkle of the

bracelet. He snatched it up, scooping two chocolate bars at the same time.

"My share," he said, grinning. He held up the bracelet to admire. "Someone will like this." His voice held a gloating note, and the boy's wide mouth twisted with helpless fury.

"May God make you too limp to enjoy her!"

"What else?" said the man, ignoring the insult, his eyes hot with anger, but hotter still with greed. He held out his hand toward the boy on the floor, palm up, the fingers moving invitingly. Hani and Farida gazed at him, willing themselves not to glance at the yogurt pot.

"Give."

A step outside the door broke the tension.

"Farida, where are you? Have you heard? The Sultan's envoy has arrived at last! A Cup Companion himself! They say he is searching for someone!" a voice cried from the doorway. "He is visiting every room. Come out and see!"

Her eyes liquid with terror, Farida stared at Hani. But it was impossible to get rid of the wallet now.

"Good morning, Rashid, morning Mrs. Rashid," the camp director said cheerfully. "What's the story here, Alison?"

His assistant wiped her damp forehead, replaced her hat and consulted the sheaf of documents on her clipboard. "Rashid al Hamza Muntazer, his wife, seven children. Joharis. We don't have their exact ages, but the nurse has estimated them as all under twelve."

Sharif Azad al Dauleh, Cup Companion to the Sultan of Bagestan, touched his fist to his heart in respectful greeting to the family. The brief conversation that followed differed little from thousands of others he had heard over the past weeks. *Please tell them the children should be in school, that my wife is very depressed. I am a construction engineer. I want to work. Please ask them how long we will be kept here.*

The group moved on, the anguish ringing in his ears. As at every camp, it was the same tale of nightmare and waste, endlessly repeated. Each one a variation of hell on earth.

They had covered over half of the detention centre now, and Sharif had almost despaired of finding the boy. His instinct told him that a child as wily as that would have some hiding place, and having stolen Sharif's wallet—a fact which Sharif had discovered without surprise when he returned to the car—he had every reason to hide to avoid a meeting.

But it was imperative that he find the boy again.

At the next door, a Bagestani woman held a baby, another child clutching her skirt.

"This is Mrs. Sabzi," the assistant read aloud. "She has three children—a son, Hani, a daughter, Jamila, and the baby."

Sharif brought a fist to his breast and bowed.

"Excellency." Farida returned the salute, then stood rocking the baby and looking anxiously at him. Her eyes wide with fascination, the baby reached one hand to the Cup Companion, letting go of her teething ring.

The blue rubber teething ring that he had last seen under his own foot on the highway.

Sharif smiled. *Got you!* he told the boy mentally, putting out a finger to the baby, who clutched it and fixed him with a heart-rending look.

"You have a son, Mrs. Sabzi?" he asked.

Alarm darkened her eyes, and she licked her lips. "I—yes, my son, Hani."

Sharif smiled. "May I meet him?"

"Excellency, you are very kind! It is good of you, but you are an important man and my son…" She shrugged to show how unimportant her son was.

Sharif inclined his head. "If he is here, I would like to meet him."

"Alas, he is not well, Excellency! I have told him to stay in bed, though he was very eager to meet you. We are Sabzi people, Excellency, from the islands," she said brightly, in an obvious effort to turn the conversation.

"Is your son here now?"

"Yes—no!" the woman began, and then her eyes moved, and her small gasp made Sharif look towards the door of her room. There was the boy, gazing straight at him with an accuse-and-be-damned look. He limped towards his mother and she put an arm around his shoulder, drawing him against her.

"Here is Hani, Excellency!" she said, her voice going up an octave, though she tried to appear calm. "You see he is not so ill that he will stay in bed when a Cup Companion of the Sultan visits!"

She looked anxiously between Sharif and the boy as if expecting him to denounce the boy, and almost wept in relief when instead he said, "You say you are from the Gulf Islands?"

"Yes, Excellency. Our home was the island of Solomon's Foot. They destroyed our house and drove us out of the island. My husband was arrested. Fifteen months, Excellency, and I have heard no news of him!"

"The Sultan's people are working to reunite all political prisoners with their families. I hope you will soon hear news of your husband, Mrs. Sabzi."

"But here we are so far away! Many, many thousand miles, they say. How will my husband find us? Please tell the Sultan that we want to come home."

Unless she was a miracle of preservation, she was not old enough to be the boy's mother. Sharif's gaze raked her face for a resemblance to the boy. Family connections were often constructs in the camps, partly because of Western ignorance of the importance of certain relationships in other cultures, partly because distant relationships increased in importance when many family members had been lost. So great-uncles became fathers, and second cousins became brothers and sisters, to satisfy the requirements of an alien authority.

But he could see no trace of family resemblance at all.

"Your husband, Mrs. Sabzi…" he began.

"I think you have dropped something, Excellency," the boy interrupted.

The mother choked with alarm.

Sharif glanced down to see his wallet lying against his foot. The boy bent to retrieve it, straightened and, with a level, challenging look, offered it to him.

The director blinked. "Is that *your* wallet?" he cried in English. "How did it get there?"

"It must have fallen from my pocket," Sharif replied.

"I doubt it very much," said the director dryly. "You'd better check to see what's missing."

"Shokran," Sharif said to the boy. *Thank you.* He took the wallet, his fingers brushing the boy's with a jolting awareness of his painful thinness. Why didn't this woman who called herself his mother take better care of her adopted son? And what were the camp authorities about, to allow a child to starve like this?

Sharif flipped the wallet open. The cash was gone. He understood the boy's deliberate, self-destructive challenge, but instead of anger he felt a deep sorrow.

"Everything accounted for," he said quietly, pocketing the wallet.

"Excellency, you are a good man!" the mother exploded in a rush of relief, lifted her arm from the boy's shoulders, seized his hand and kissed it. "We are simple people, and life is so empty here. Our house must be rebuilt, but we are ready for hard work. Only tell us that we may go home!" The boy, meanwhile, looked stunned. His eyes were black with confusion and mistrust as he gazed at Sharif. Kindness completely unsettled him, and that, too, flooded Sharif's heart with sadness.

Three

$\mathbf{H}$ani sat on a rock and gazed out over the barren plain in the profound darkness, his stomach aching with a hunger that was not for food. A light breeze was blowing from the mountains. The air was dry, with the desert dust and the astringent perfume of a plant whose name he didn't know combining to create the familiar scent of desolation. Stars glittered in the black, new moon sky overhead, their alien configurations reminding him how far away from home he was. Along the distant highway now and then long fingers of light dragged a lone car through the darkness. The town lay fragmented on the distant horizon, a broken wineglass catching the starlight.

Everything else was night. Behind him, the camp had a ghostly glow, throwing barbed wire shadows on the desert floor, but the rock where he sat hidden shrouded the thin figure.

For the first time in a long time, Hani was thinking about the past. The stranger's voice had stirred memories in him.

Those strange memories he didn't understand—of a handsome man, a smiling woman…other children. In those memories he had a different name.

Your name is Hani. Forget that other name. You must forget.

He had been obedient to the command. Mostly he had forgotten. In the dim and distant memory that was all that remained—or was it a dream?—life was a haze of gentle shade, cool fountains, and flowers.

She had played in a beautiful courtyard by a reflecting pool, amid the luscious scent of roses carried from flower beds that surrounded it on all sides. In that pool the house was perfectly reflected, its beautiful fluted dome, its tiled pillars, the arched balconies. When the sun grew hot, there were fountains. Water droplets were carried on the breeze to fall against her face and hair.

Now, in this water-starved world, he could still remember the feeling of delight.

And then one day the fountain was silent. He remembered that, and her brother—was it her brother?—his face stretched and pale. *There are only two of us now,* he had said, holding her tight. *I'll look after you.*

Will we watch the fountains again? she had asked, and though her brother had not answered, she knew. They had stayed alone in the silent house, she didn't know how long. One morning she had awakened to find herself in a strange place and her brother gone.

You must be a boy now, they had told her. *Your name is Hani.* And when she protested that she already had a name, *Forget your old name. That is all gone. Your brother is gone. We are your family now, we will look after you. See, here are your new brothers and sisters.*

And he had forgotten the name. He became Hani, a boy, without ever knowing why, and the old life faded. He had shared a bedroom with four others in a small, hot apartment that had no pool, no fountains, no rose beds. If he asked about such things, his stepmother first pretended not to hear, and then, if Hani persisted, grew angry.

Who were the people he remembered? His heart said the tall man was his father, the smiling woman his mother, the other children his sisters and brothers, whose names he could, sometimes, almost remember.

No. We are your family. Here are your sisters and brothers.

Something about the stranger made him remember that life long since disappeared, that life that he had been forbidden to remember. The memory ached in him, as fresh as if the loss were the only one he had suffered, as if the dark years since had never blunted the edge of that grief with more and then more.

The stranger's voice had been like the voices he had heard long ago, like his father's, summoning up another world.

Don't think about that, don't say anything. You must forget….

Was it a dream only? Had his childish, unhappy mind made it all up? And yet he remembered his father and mother smiling at him, remembered a cocoon of love.

One day, when you are older, you must know the truth. But not now…

And then it was too late. After the bomb, his stepmother had stared at Hani helplessly before she died, her eyes trying to convey the message that her torn, bleeding throat could not speak.

Who were they, the people whose faces he remembered, the memory of whose love sometimes, in the bleakness of a loveless existence, had surged up from the depths of his heart to remind him of what was possible? Where was that home, that he could sometimes see so clearly in his mind's eye, and why was it all suddenly so fresh before him now?

In the nearest thing to a luxury hotel the town had, Sharif Azad al Dauleh stood on a darkened balcony, a phone to his ear, waiting to hear the Sultan's voice. Although the desert air was cool, he was naked except for the towel around his hips. Above it the smoke-bronze skin, the long, straight back, the

lean-muscled stomach, arms and chest gave him the look of
a genie from a particularly beautiful lamp.

"I offer you a mission," the Sultan had said.

The manservant had brought a tray of cool drinks as the
Sultan bent over a document file and opened it. Tall glasses
of juice had been poured out and set down, a dish of nuts arranged, invisible traces of nothing at all removed with the expert flick of a white cloth.

On top of the thin sheaf of documents was the photograph of a young child, a girl. Ashraf slipped it off the pile
and handed it to Sharif, then sat back, picked up his glass
and drank.

The Cup Companion examined the photograph. The child's
eyes gazed at him, trusting and happy, with the unmistakable,
fine bone structure around the eyes that was the hallmark of
the al Jawadi. Sharif knew that members of the royal family
were still surfacing from every point on the globe, but this
child he had never seen.

"My cousin, Princess Shakira," Sultan Ashraf had murmured.

Sharif waited.

"She is the daughter of my cousin Mahlouf. Uncle Safa's
son."

Sharif's thick eyelashes flicked with surprise. Among the
first of the royal family to be assassinated by Ghasib after the
coup, it was Prince Safa whose death had prompted the old
Sultan to command all his heirs to take assumed names and
go into hiding. This was the first Sharif had heard that Prince
Safa had left descendants, but anything was possible.

"Safa had a child by his first wife—the singer Suhaila."

"I had no idea that Safa had been married to Bagestan's
Nightingale!"

"Few did. It was an ill-fated, short-lived marriage, when
he was very young. She left him while she was still pregnant. In later years, although a connection was kept up, the
public was not aware that Prince Safa was Mahlouf's fa-

ther. But the files of Ghasib's secret police prove that they knew. Mahlouf, with his wife and family, died in a traffic accident in the late eighties. We now learn that it was no accident."

A muscle tightened in Sharif's jaw as he glanced at the document Ashraf handed him. By its markings, it had been culled from the files of the dictator's secret police. Mechanically he noted the code name of the agent who had masterminded the assassination.

"We have this man, Lord," he said in grim satisfaction.

"So I have been informed. But that isn't the issue here. A child escaped. We had always believed that the whole family was killed in the accident. But these files suggest that we were wrong, and that Mahlouf's youngest daughter, Shakira, was not in the car. The secret police got wind of this rumour, but apparently never managed to trace her.

"We've now received independent confirmation of the rumour, from someone who says Shakira was secretly adopted by the dissident activist Arif al Vafa Bahrami."

"Barakullah!" Sharif sat up, blinking.

"Yes, he was even more loyal than we knew. But we have no further information. Bahrami escaped to England, and the family was there for years, waiting for their appeal for asylum to be heard, before Arif was assassinated in the street," Ash said. "If the story is true, Shakira should have been with them. But there's no record of a child with that name."

"Would they have given her a different name?" Sharif suggested.

"Maybe." The Sultan leaned back in his chair and sighed. "But there are compelling arguments against the idea, Sharif. After Arif Bahrami's death the British Home Office ruled that his wife and children were no longer at risk and must return to Bagestan. There was an appeal. We've now received the transcript of that appeal from the British government. Arif's wife made no mention of harbouring a descendant of the Sultan. Yet such information would surely have strengthened the family's case for being allowed to stay."

"The child would have gone straight onto Ghasib's death list," Sharif pointed out. "And not merely Princess Shakira—the whole family would have been in danger." He paused and took a sip of juice, set down his glass. "What was the result of the appeal?"

"It failed. The family were deported from Britain."

Sharif's lips tightened into grimness.

"They were accepted by Parvan, however, and went there—not long before the Kaljuk invasion."

The Sultan absently tidied the file, putting the photograph on top. He sat for a moment with his hands framing it, gazing down on his young cousin's face.

"Records from Parvan show the name Bahrami in a refugee camp that was bombed during the Kaljuk War. Survivors apparently went to an Indonesian refugee camp, but after that records are chaotic. Someone who might be one of the Bahrami children appears among the records of orphans there, but that camp was closed down."

He leaned back and rubbed his eyes.

"The inhabitants were then shipped to camps all over the world. The trail goes completely cold."

Sharif picked up the photograph again. It showed a child four or five years old. Dark hair that tumbled down over her shoulders, glossy and curling. Rounded cheeks glowing with health and vitality, wide, thoughtful eyes, and a mischievous smile.

If ever he had a daughter, he thought irrelevantly, he would like her to look like this.

"How old is she now?" he asked.

"If the records we have are correct, twenty-one."

"She has the al Jawadi look, all right."

Ashraf nodded. "Yes."

The Cup Companion, still gazing at the child's face, was

suddenly conscious of a powerful draw. He wondered what kind of woman she had grown into. If she had lived.

"You want me to find her?" he said.

"Yes. Or, more probably, some evidence of what her fate was. And yet, if there's any hope... God knows how many camps you'll have to visit. It's a nearly hopeless task, Sharif. I know it."

Sharif sat for a moment, accepting it with a slow nod. Then the two men got to their feet and embraced again. "Do your best. It may be impossible," said the Sultan.

The mouth that some people thought cold had stretched in a quick smile. His hand had formed a fist at his heart.

"By my head and eyes, Lord," Sheikh Sharif Azad al Dauleh had said. "If the Princess is alive, I'll find her."

"Sharif."

"Lord."

"What news?"

"Something's come up here, Ash."

"You've got a line on her?"

"Not the Princess," Sharif said. "Lord, brace yourself for something strange. I've found someone else here. I thought—"

"Someone *else?*"

"A boy, about fourteen or fifteen." Far out in the desert, a distant glow pinpointed the detention centre. "An orphan, I imagine—he's attached himself to a family that's obviously not his own. If he's not an al Jawadi, Ash, then neither are you. Any idea who he might be?"

There was the silence of shock being absorbed. Then he heard the Sultan's breath escape in a rush.

"*Allah,* how can I say? We know so little about some branches of the family, and yet...might someone have mistaken the name? Or could it be that *two* of Mahlouf's children escaped?"

"The boy speaks English, which would fit what we know of the Bahramis' history." Sharif hesitated. "He would have been a babe in arms at the time of the assassination."

In the shadows on the table behind him, the file on Princess Shakira lay open. Sharif turned and picked up the photograph. Somewhere along the line he had become committed to finding this child alive. To knowing the woman she had become. He didn't want to accept that this delightful, elusive little spirit had been wiped from the earth without having the chance to flower.

It was nothing but sentiment, and he knew well that he would have despised it in others. He despised it in himself. Many members of the royal family had been assassinated during the years of Ghasib's rule, and countless other innocents. Why should he want to pull this one out of the darkness that had descended on his country thirty years before?

If it was the boy who'd been saved…had he been looking for the wrong person all along?

"What does the boy himself say?" Ash's voice brought him out of the reverie.

"I haven't asked, Lord. He's been deeply affected by what he's been through." The image of the boy's face, so stamped with grief and suffering, rose in his mind. Apart from the al Jawadi characteristics the two shared, the contrast between Hani and the little girl in the photograph covered everything, Sharif reflected sadly—she was trusting, where the boy trusted none; she was happy, while the boy suffered; she was nourished, the boy starved; she believed, the boy had learned cynicism. And yet they were connected by that one thread, which seemed to overpower all the differences. The family resemblance dominated.

"I'd like your permission to bring him home without first trying to establish his background. To raise his hopes and then leave him in these conditions because he proves not to be what I think—"

"No, of course we can't do that. Do whatever your judgement suggests, Sharif."

When he hung up, the Cup Companion remained where he was, staring out over the desert. Smoke trailed up from the thin cigar in his hand, its shape twisting and scudding before his absent eyes.

Sharif Azad al Dauleh was variously said to be cold, cynical, selfish, too intelligent for his own good, but none of those accusations hit the mark. Sharif was highly intelligent, and proud of a noble lineage. He was also courageous and impatient of weakness or cowardice. Weaker men—and women—might well resent such a combination. But if his compassion was rarely roused, it was perhaps because he first had none for himself.

He had seen a great deal of human suffering during the weeks of his fruitless search. And only now did he feel the weight of helplessness that he had been unconsciously carrying with him.

Was it because the boy was so obviously an al Jawadi and Sharif's loyalty was bred in the bone? Was it something in Hani himself? Or was this child—with his haunted eyes and his cynical understanding that he was destined to be one of the world's dispossessed, a child who'd had nothing for so long he didn't remember what something was—simply the last straw of weight Sharif's spirit could bear?

Was it that he was finally doing something, however small? He would save one soul, pluck one suffering child from the nightmare of wasted, desolate life he saw.

Sharif suddenly felt how much of a toll the weeks of bearing witness to so much suffering had taken on his inner reserves.

He was glad to be going home. He needed a breather.

"Home?" Hani whispered. "Take me home?"

The vision of the fountain trembled before his mind's eye, and his heart thudded with hope.

Sharif realized his mistake. This was the most difficult interview he had ever conducted, and he hoped he would never have another like it.

"Home to Bagestan."

But the child was lost in a dream. "Is my mother there? My father?"

Sharif swallowed. *Allah,* what had made him think he could handle this himself? "I don't think so, Hani."

"They died," Hani agreed, hollowly. For a long moment the boy gazed at him, with an expression almost of worship in the dark, hungry eyes. "Are you my brother?" he whispered.

The question shook him.

"No," he said gently. "I am not your brother."

Hani bit his lip to hold back the sudden, urgent tears.

"Who am I? Do you know who I am?"

"I'm sorry, Hani. All I have are questions, like you. If there is anything you can tell me, it may help to find out who you are. Do you remember any names?"

He hadn't meant to start like this. His plan had been to say the minimum possible—only what was necessary to get the boy aboard the plane. But in the face of such a deep and urgent need to know, his resolve failed.

The eyes were liquid with sadness as Hani shook his head. "I had to forget all the names, when I was very small. I don't remember any, not even my brothers' and sisters'. They said someone would kill me if I spoke the names. A bad man."

Sharif struggled to keep what he felt from showing on his face. Although there had been many victims, only one group of people in Bagestan had been in danger from Ghasib on the strength of name alone—members of the royal family.

"Who said it?"

"My—she said she was my mother, but I knew she wasn't. I always thought of her, in my heart, as my stepmother. But I wasn't allowed to say so."

A strange, powerful silence surrounded them. Outside the director's office the usual sounds of the camp were dimmed, as though the air had become too thin to carry them.

"What was your stepfamily's name?"

Hani was holding his breath. The world seemed to still its

own breath with his. Somehow, even before he spoke the name, he sensed that this one word had the power to change everything.

"Bahrami," he breathed.

The name fell into the silence like a cut diamond into a still pond.

This time Sharif could not stifle his reaction, because every atom of body and soul was electrified. He could only stare at the boy.

"Bahrami." He repeated the word softly. "Arif al Vafa Bahrami."

"Yes!"

Suddenly all the torment of his missing past boiled up in him.

"Tell me! Tell me who they were! A man and a woman, and other children, and a house with a fountain. Roses and…so many roses. Who were they?"

Sharif swallowed hard. Pity, he found, tore at the heart with eagle's claws.

"Hani, I think—please understand that we can't be sure—that your father might have been Mahlouf Jawad al Nadim. Does the—"

His heart kicked so hard his body jerked. Shivers ran over his skin. "My father? Is that my father's name? Is he—is he alive, then? Did he send you to find me?"

"I'm sorry, Hani, no. He died many years ago. Does the name sound familiar?"

He shook his head, half blinded by tears. Was that his name, his father's name, words he didn't know at all? "Why don't I know it, if it was my father's name? My own name," he added softly, and then repeated it, as if to test the flavour. "Mahlouf Jawad al Nadim. My father."

"You must have been very young when they died," he suggested consolingly. "Maybe you never knew it."

Sharif turned to his briefcase and drew out the Princess Shakira file. Watched by Hani with huge dark eyes, he opened it. "I want to show you a photograph," he said quietly. "It may be that she was also living with the Bahramis. Do you remember this face?"

He drew out the photograph and set it in front of Hani on the low table, watching the boy's face closely, noting the terrible differences that hunger, horror and deprivation had created in two faces with such a strong family resemblance.

The child was silent a long time, staring at the picture. Then one tiny jewel teardrop fell, and landed on Princess Shakira's cheek. It lay on the photograph quivering and sparkling in a ray of sun. Hani looked up into Sharif's face, swallowed, and wiped his cheek with one thin hand.

"What was her name?" the boy whispered. "What was her name?"

Sharif saw it then, finally. Not a strong family resemblance, no. Much more than that. Now that he saw it, it only amazed him that it had taken so long.

He spoke very, very softly, as if the air itself might break.

"Shakira," he said. "Your name is—Shakira."

Four

"Shakira."

The name seemed to rush all around the room, crazily, like a whirlwind, before striking her heart a powerful, staggering blow. Her mouth opened in a slow, soundless gasp.

A spiral of light burned in her, wrapping her heart, spinning outward to warm her whole being and blast through the coldness of years, light the darkness, fill the emptiness. She stood up without knowing it, gazing at Sharif, then down at the photograph, then at Sharif again.

"Shakira." She said it again, and then, inside, she heard what she had yearned and strained to hear for so many years: her mother's voice speaking her own true name. And she saw the fountain as if it were there in front of her, blocking out the drab office with its ugly, utilitarian furniture; and the scent of water, the wonderful scent of water on desert air, and of roses trembling under the droplets and releasing their perfumes, flooded her whole being.

Shakira. She heard her mother's voice in her ears. *My own rose.*

She knew that it was true—this picture was her, and her name was Shakira. And she *had* been loved—once, long ago. It was not a memory her wishes had invented. It was true. The memories of love were true. She had had a family and they had loved her.

The tears welled up and poured over her cheeks in an abundance Sharif would not have believed possible. He had never seen such a flood from any creature's eyes, and it made him think of some old, half-forgotten fairy tale where the princess wept a lake and then sailed away on it.

Her drowned eyes glittering like black diamonds behind the tears, she looked up at him, begging, "Who am I? Please, who am I?"

He hadn't meant any of this to happen. His intention had been to leave the Sultan and his family to deal with the whole delicate issue of identity and reclamation. But, however unintentionally, he had created this moment. He could not deny her now. He could not add to the intolerable suffering of years with even another day's delay.

"You—" He discovered that he could hardly speak for the choke of feeling in his own throat. He coughed and swallowed and tried again. "Your full name is Shakira Warda Jawad al Nadim."

"Why did you come for me? Who wants me? My family is all dead."

Her black diamond eyes pierced him with such longing to be contradicted that his own heart nearly broke.

"No. Your own closest family are gone, but there are others. You have a large family of cousins, aunts and uncles," Sharif began.

A wail tore from her throat, a howl that shook him in his deepest being, for it was the cry of release from a terrible, unimaginable grief. The child leapt to her feet, the noise still pouring from her throat as the tears from her eyes, as though nothing could stop the flood. She flung herself against his chest, her hands clutching folds of his kaftan as if to shake the truth from him, and the flooded eyes gazed up into his.

"Cousins? I have cousins, aunts, uncles? My own, my own family? They know who I am?" she demanded.

Someone opened the door of the office and a curious head peered around it at him, but with a frown Sharif sent the fool scuttling back, and they were alone again. He gently set his hands on the thin little shoulders as emotion racked her body.

"They are waiting to welcome you home."

A thousand memories welled up inside Shakira now, potent and irresistible, a flood of grief and joy, as if the sound of her own name had unlocked a door behind which everything had been hidden. The faces of her father and mother, her brothers and sisters, flashed in her mind, one after another, all together. The house, the fountain, the rose garden, the beauty that had once surrounded her. Music. A book, with the picture of a prince and princess in gorgeous robes on a flying horse, high over a city of domes and minarets.

Voices. Her name, and others. A jumble of sensation and emotion that overwhelmed her. Those who had loved her, whom she had been forced to forget.

The memories flooded through her, and the memory of happiness, filling her so powerfully with both pain and joy that she felt she couldn't hold it all.

When the storm had passed, she wiped her face with her hands and her T-shirt, and gazed hungrily up into his face.

"Are you my cousin?" she asked, yearning for a connection with him that would make her homecoming immediate. "Are you my family?"

Family. The word had a ring that he had never heard before, like a starving man pronouncing *bread*. An unfamiliar protectiveness welled up in him, and he wished he could be the person she wanted him to be.

"I am not related to you. I was sent to find you by your cousin, who is the head of your family. He has only just learned that you are alive. Until now, he believed that you had died in the accident with your parents."

"He thought I was dead?" She gazed at him. "Who is my cousin? What is his name? Why didn't he come to find me himself?"

Sharif pressed his lips together, and said slowly, "I think the answer to your questions will be a…an even bigger surprise to you. Your father was related to a very important Bagestani family."

Her eyes showed such a kaleidoscope of doubt, incredulity and suspicion that Sharif could almost have laughed.

"Important?" she repeated, the child who had been among the forgotten of humanity for nearly ten years.

It was probably stupid to tell her like this, but the situation had been created now, and it was impossible not to go on.

"Mahlouf Jawad al Nadim was the grandson of the last Sultan. Your cousin is Ashraf al Jawadi, the newly crowned Sultan of Bagestan. Shakira, you—you are a princess."

The polished domes and minarets of Medinat al Bostan gleamed in the afternoon sun as they flew in, hazy and shimmering, a dream city. The blue, turquoise and purple-tiled dome was the Old Palace, now restored, Sharif told her, to its former use as the home of the Sultan, and to its former name, the Jawad Palace.

"Like me," said Shakira.

The Shah Jawad Mosque was a dome of burnished gold at the opposite end of a green and beautiful square that was the heart of the city. Under Ghasib it had been made into a museum. That, too, had been restored to its former use.

The templates had faded in her heart, like a dream that cannot be held. She had been so young when she had been torn from her home. The reality of life in the camps had battered the memory, for how could such beauty exist in the world side by side with what she knew?

Now it was as if a magic hand restored the dream images in all their glorious perfection of colour and shape, and her heart leapt with feeling. Home. At long last she was home.

"Will I see my family there?" she had asked during the long, interminable hours of waiting, while Farida and her little girl talked and laughed and ran to and fro, astonished at the jet's unabashed luxury, as the stewardess showed them around.

Shakira had not joined them. She sat in her seat opposite Sharif with a grave face, her eyes dark with a mix of emotions. Against the background of the lavishly fitted jet, one of Ghasib's private fleet that was being used by the Sultan's government now, the marks of the Princess's life of deprivation were thrown into sharp relief. The painfully thin body, the ragged, sunburnt hair, the cheap boy's clothes, and, most of all, the haunted eyes were a reproach to the background of opulence. No one, he thought, could have looked less like a princess of the ruling house.

"Some of them," he had assured her. "Everyone who can. Many have not returned to Bagestan yet."

"Some," she repeated, who had none. *"Many."*

"Yes, that is how you will number your family in future."

Nothing in his life had ever pulled at his heart as did this desperate child's anguished yearning for someone to call her own.

"My cousins." She breathed deeply. "Will you tell me about my family?"

Of course he told her. "Your great-grandfather Sultan Hafzuddin had three wives, Rabia, Sonia and Maryam. Between them they had many children and grandchildren…."

Shakira had sat wide-eyed, drinking it in like water in a desert, the story of her heritage. "My grandmother was a famous singer?" she said when he stopped.

Sharif nodded. "Her professional name was Suha, and she

was very beautiful. She went into exile in protest at the time of Ghasib's coup. Your cousins are searching for her now."

"Oh!" Her gaze drifted into the middle distance and he saw what softness memories of her early life gave to the stern little face. "I—we visited someone once. She wore gold bracelets, and she let me put them on and told me one day I'd be a beautiful woman with bracelets of my own." A tear fell from one eye, and she brushed it away as if it shamed her, then fixed a stern gaze on him. "Who else?"

"Rabia had another son, Wafiq. It is his eldest son, Ashraf, your father's cousin, who is now the Sultan," he said. "The Sultan has a brother, Haroun, and three sisters, Aliyah and Iman and Lina. Ash and Haroun are married, and their wives are Dana and Mariel."

"Do I really have so many family?" she whispered, half to herself.

"Yes, and more. Since the Return, many are coming back to Bagestan. Queen Sonia's granddaughters, Noor and Jalia, are about your age, and both are now engaged to Cup Companions. Their cousin Najib and his wife also live close. You have almost too many to count."

She wasn't satisfied until he had described them all, told her everything he could. At the end, she had stayed motionless and silent for minutes, as if still listening to what it meant.

A massive series of buildings in black and white marble came into view, looking alien and clumsy against the ancient perfection of the delicate arches and domes, and Shakira frowned.

"What is that?" she asked Sharif, pointing.

He glanced at her, half smiling at her wondering indignation. "That is the New Palace compound. Ghasib hired foreign architects. It took years to complete—it may not have been finished when you left Bagestan."

"It looks like the sugar cubes from a relief plane at one of the camps," she observed. "A huge box broke and the sugar spilled everywhere in the mud, in piles. We stood around, watching it dissolve into the earth, wondering who had sent us sugar cubes. Men shouted, 'But where is the mint tea to go with it?' The little children were so hungry, they couldn't be stopped from eating it, and the mud, too. It was filthy. Many got dysentery as a result. Some died."

Sharif listened, knowing that there were many such stories behind the tragic eyes, which now fixed him with urgent demand. "Why did they do that? We needed flour for bread, we needed food. Why did they send us sugar cubes? Men said it was a deliberate insult, to show us that the world did not care."

"Bureaucracy creates many such stupidities," he said, shaking his head in despair, for how was that an explanation?

She gazed out the window again as the New Palace disappeared behind them.

"Why didn't he make something beautiful?"

Sharif laughed aloud, for the New Palace, when it was built, had been hailed as the architect's "creative modernist blending of the influences of East and West." But as with the emperor's clothes, the child was right. It was a solidly ugly fortress, white marble notwithstanding.

"Ghasib was a modernist. He admired the architecture of the West. It would not look so grotesque in the capitals of Europe, perhaps."

"No, because everything is grotesque there!" Shakira agreed emphatically. "What do they know of living? There they keep fresh water in their toilets! Did you know that? You pee into a big bowl of water! What waste! In the camps when I was thirsty and there was no water, I used to tell myself, well, today you are not drinking the water that you wasted in the toilet in England on May the sixteenth. And tomorrow there will be no water again, and then you will not drink what you wasted on May the seventeenth."

She spoke as one who has returned to a place of sanity after years in the asylum, and he grieved a little, for those who expect perfection, even of a newly reborn country striving for the best, are doomed to disappointment. Sharif knew for a fact that there were flush toilets in the Jawad Palace. He wondered how Ash and the rest of the family would react to this little firebrand coming among them, with her uncompromising vision and straight talk.

Farida and Jamila sat down beside them. They were coming in to land, and it was not necessary for him to give her an answer. The stewardess began helping Farida fasten her belt, and Sharif did the same for Jamila. Shakira disdained help. Asking for help would be to show weakness.

"And now you will live in a palace and be a princess!" Farida said, to fill the empty waiting time before landing. Her voice held no trace of envy. "To think that my son was a princess all the time!"

She laughed loudly. "My husband will not believe it when I tell him. Oh, Excellency, how wonderful it will be to go home! Will my husband be there? Perhaps he is already building the house again. He is a very good provider. We pick and dry medicinal herbs to sell on the mainland. What a good husband he is! Are you married, Excellency?"

"It has not been God's will to send me a wife yet," he replied, in the polite formula of the country folk.

"*Insh'Allah,* it will soon please Him. When you marry, I am sure you will be good to your wife. The prophet said, *A man is known by the way he treats his wife.* If you are as good a husband as mine is, your wife will be very happy, and Allah will bless you with many children."

"Your husband chose the mother of his children well," Sharif said. "I am sure he knows it."

They were speaking as though her husband would be found alive, and *insh'Allah* he would be. But whether he was alive or not, found or not, for the moment there would be no return to Solomon's Foot, a fact Sharif had not so far explained to Farida, and he was hoping not to have to.

"You will wish to visit at the palace with the Princess while your husband is searched for," he remarked. "The Sultan asked me to extend his warm welcome to the adopted family of his cherished cousin."

Farida smiled broadly, shaking her head, and patted Shakira's arm. "The Princess has her own family now, and I have mine. It is fitting that each return where we belong. I do not belong in the palace, but in my home."

"It will take your husband time to rebuild."

"And is not my place there, helping him?" Farida countered, polite but determined.

Sharif cleared his throat uncomfortably. It hadn't occurred to any of them that the woman would turn down even a short visit to the palace.

He was aware that Shakira was watching him closely. He smiled reassuringly at her, but he was saved from the searching question he could see in her eyes by Jamila. The little girl was sitting in the seat beside his, and now she lifted her chin and looked up into his face.

"Where is my Amina?" she asked sadly. "Do you have her?"

"Who is Amina?" Sharif dutifully enquired.

"Oh, Jamila," Farida scolded gently. "How could His Excellency have your doll? He was not there that day! She lost her doll when they arrested my husband and took us from our home, Excellency. What a terrible day it was! And she has not forgotten. It was a doll I made her myself. I have told her, as soon as we have built the new house, I will make her another. It only needs one of my husband's old socks, Excellency, and some coloured wool."

"I want my Amina!" said the child mulishly.

Sharif leaned down to her. "There are many beautiful dolls in the city. Will you come to the bazaar with me and choose a new Amina?"

Setting her mouth in a determined negative, Jamila silently turned her head from side to side. Her soft hair brushed up against the high chair-back like a cat's fur, and Sharif laughed.

"Do not speak so when someone offers you a gift!" her mother admonished.

"I didn't speak," the child protested, and they all laughed.

The plane taxied to a stop at a distance from the main terminal building, where a small marble-and-gold pavilion had been built for welcoming foreign dignitaries and VIPs out of the public eye. As they waited for the steps to be rolled into position a dozen people emerged from the building and came towards the plane.

Shakira had never seen such beautiful people. Men and women with sparkling eyes, smiling faces, flowing hair that gleamed in the hot sunshine. Their clothes were a mass of brilliant colours, and white so bright it blinded her. Even in her dreams she had not been able to imagine such a whiteness.

"Who are they?" she whispered, turning to Sharif.

"They are your family." A stern-looking man in a white djellaba and green keffiyeh and a magnificently beautiful woman with black hair like a cloud down her back walked together, leading the group. They were tall and straight, and she couldn't seem to look away from them.

"The Sultan and Sultana," said Sharif. "Your cousins."

Something kicked in her chest.

The door of the aircraft opened at last, and Shakira stood for a moment looking out into the brilliant sunshine, at all the strangers who were not strangers. She swallowed, dropped her head, and tried to breathe, but her chest was too tight. She felt as if she were dying. She, who prided herself on her fearlessness. She had defied angry security men in shops, she had leapt from moving trucks...but now fear choked her.

She turned blindly towards Sharif, standing a few yards away, watching her with grave eyes and a mouth that was half smiling. Unconsciously she stretched out her hand to him, and he felt it as if tiny yearning tendrils reached for his heart.

"You come with me," she pleaded.

The Cup Companion stepped over to her. "They are your family, Shakira," he said, gently turning her to the door. "They are waiting for you."

She looked out. They were all there. Her family. Her *family*. The little crowd called and waved to her, and she heard her name, her true name, on a dozen smiling lips. It was pronounced with love, as if she were someone precious, someone to cherish.

"Shakira!" they cried. "Welcome home, Shakira!"

Five

A sweet wind was blowing, bringing the soft smells of the desert to her nostrils. The heat was dry; her tears evaporated even as they formed on her cheeks.

The tall, dark man in the white djellaba, his green keffiyeh lifting in the breeze, moved to the foot of the steps and stood looking gravely up at her. And with a blow that struck her heart, Shakira recognized the eyes in the stern, noble face.

A wordless cry warbled from her throat, and she dashed down the steps and stopped in front of him.

"Who are you?" she whispered. "Are you—"

"I am your cousin Ashraf," said the Sultan simply.

"Oh, you look like my father!" she cried, and that other, beloved face was sharp and clear in her memory, as it had not been for too long.

Shakira stood for a moment, not knowing how to deal with the powerful feelings that rose up in her. After a lifetime without closeness she had no instinctive way to express the overwhelming mixture of love, joy, pain and almost terrifying relief.

Ashraf broke the tension by wrapping her in a tight embrace. "Welcome home, Cousin," he said.

For a moment she resisted, her thin body tensing as if for an attack. Then a strange, unfamiliar sensation burst up, driving a sob into her throat: the human comfort of touch. Hot tears burned her eyes, too powerful to resist, though deep instinct told her it showed a dangerous weakness.

Crying in front of so many people! How they would treat her now—they would take all the drinking water, steal her food! And yet—the arms around her felt so safe, like something she remembered feeling, long ago....

Before she had time to sort out such conflicting emotions, Ashraf released her to be embraced again, this time by the magnificently beautiful woman with the cloud of black hair, whom she had seen from the plane.

"I'm Dana, Ash's wife," Shakira heard. "Welcome! We are so happy and thankful to have found you at last. What a terrible time you've had! But you're safe with your family now."

Hani had always been able to contain his tears. Sometimes he had felt that his soul was so dry tears would never happen to him again. In the camps that was a good thing.

Shakira, though, could not stop her tears. From that moment of learning her true name, she seemed to have lost her power over her emotions, over the feeling that flooded from her eyes. And now, held in the tall Sultana's embrace, head against her breasts, as her mother had held her long ago, and no one since, Shakira was overwhelmed.

"You're safe here," the Sultana said again, as if she understood everything. "It's all right."

The Sultana's gently smiling face bent comfortingly over her, and that tore away the last vestige of self-control. Shakira wept and wept. She wept for Hani, she wept for Shakira, she wept for her loss, and she wept for her homecoming. She wept because she was torn with a confusing mix of grief and joy, and she wept for shame at her unaccustomed weakness.

She lifted her head at last, her face streaming, while her breath settled down with long, shuddering sobs. She felt ashamed, and didn't know what to say to regain face. Hastily she lifted the hem of her T-shirt to wipe her nose and face, and gave the Sultana a nervous, tentative smile.

"Oh, you are *so* like Ash!" Dana cried. "I can see how you knew her, Sharif!"

"Am I?" Shakira asked, partly because it was so completely thrilling to think that she shared a family resemblance with someone living, and partly because, even now, she doubted what was happening. Could it really be true that she was not only part of a huge family, but also that this family was the ancient royal house of Bagestan?

The others crowded round, and added their voices to the Sultana's. "Yes, look, she's just like the portrait of Grandfather's sister!"

"You've got Ash's eyes, for sure! Hi, Shakira, I'm your cousin, too! My name's Noor. Welcome to the family!"

"I don't think we'll introduce everyone now," Dana said, sensing too much tension in the thin little body under her hands. "Let's take Shakira home. She's tired from a long trip. And her foster family, too."

The Sultana turned to where Farida stood next to Sharif, Jamila clinging to her leg, the baby in her arms, and put out her hand. "We are so very grateful to you for your friendship with the Princess. Of course you will come and stay with us at the palace for as long as is necessary for us to find your husband."

Farida moved a fist to her heart and bent her head respectfully.

"Excellent Lady," she began, "I am honoured by your hospitality. Hani's place is with you, that is her home. But my home is my home, and I long to go there at once. There is no need to trouble you further. If your generosity will allow us only a little food and water for the journey, we will walk. I know the ferry boat captain—he will agree to carry us when he knows our story. My husband will pay him when he returns."

Shakira sensed rather than saw the glance that the Sultan and Sultana exchanged. Dana smiled at Farida again. "I am so sorry. There is no ferry now, and nowhere on the island for you to live. Nothing has been rebuilt yet. But you are very welcome—"

Shakira suddenly stood straighter. "Why is Farida not allowed to go home?" she demanded, the Hani in her suddenly taking the opportunity to exhibit strength after the terrible show of weakness her tears had been. "She wants to go to the island, to Solomon's Foot! Do you think to be on Solomon's Foot without a roof can be worse than to live in Burry Hill Detention Centre?"

"Cousin," the Sultan intervened, "it is not—"

Shakira could not have defined the feelings that now drove her.

"Why can't she go home?" she demanded hotly.

They all went still, looking for a way to deal with this unexpected challenge, but before anyone could muster a response, Sharif stepped out to face her, offering himself as a target. There was a kind of indrawn breath amongst those who watched, because now it was between these two, and they wondered how the Cup Companion would handle it.

She was quick to take him up on the offer. "You said you would take us home!" she accused.

Sharif met her glance firmly.

"You who have waited so many years to find your family— to find even your self, your own name, Shakira, do you imagine that everything good happens in one moment? Farida must be happy for the moment simply to be in Bagestan amongst her countrymen. She must wait a little longer to be in her own home."

"Why must she wait?"

Her fiery rage did not abash him. "She must wait because *only those who are patient shall receive their reward in full,*" he quoted gently. "Your protection of your friend does you honour, Princess, but she must submit to this."

There was a moment of silence while the thin boy-girl and the tall, strong man gazed at each other. Shakira breathed deep then, and as the strange rage passed, the tension left those watching, as if with one shared breath.

"Oh," Shakira said. She turned to Farida. "I hope it will not be long."

Farida smiled. *"Nobody can be given a blessing better and greater than patience.* Did not the Prophet himself say it?"

The young mother turned to the Sultana and bowed her head again. "Excellent Lady, I am honoured to be your guest."

In a high, blue-tiled wall an arched wooden gate opened inwards, and the little cavalcade of cars slipped from the narrow street into the courtyard within.

Shakira, in the back of a limousine between two cousins whose names were part of a jumble of names and faces, bent her head back and gazed out the rear window up at the arch as the car passed under it.

There were windows above the archway. She looked around the courtyard, where the cars were parking, one by one, in front of another, smaller archway. She guessed that it must lead out onto another street. The courtyard was faced with worn yellow brick, and the ground, too, was paved with it. Green plants lined the base of the walls, and two trees reached for the sky. Sunshine slanted down, giving the ancient brick a warm, comforting glow totally unlike the sterile structures at Burry Hill.

"Is this the palace?" she asked in wonder. "It's beautiful."

Noor chuckled a little, not unkindly, because this area was simply the private entrance and parking lot for the palace.

"You'll see how beautiful it is," she promised.

As the family clambered out of the various vehicles and urged her towards the archway, Shakira looked through, gasped and cried out, "Oh, it's like heaven!"

Beyond the arched passage was the most beautiful garden courtyard of the palace, and ever afterwards she would remember her first glimpse of it.

It was a wide rectangle, overlooked by tiers of arched balconies, and shaded with trees and ornamental shrubs, many in full flower. In the centre was a broad reflecting pool from which water bubbled up over a tall marble fountain, spilling water over its levels with a sound that was pure intoxication.

"A fountain!" she whispered. She turned to share the wonder, and saw Sharif. He was standing a little apart from the cluster of her family behind her, for they had pushed her in first, wide-eyed and speechless, to give her the garden in all its glory.

She smiled at him, her eyes alight, her gaze impelling him to her side. "Have you seen it before?" she wondered.

"Many times, Princess. My rooms are there."

He pointed up through the trees to a balcony above, from which a profusion of plants tumbled down into the magic garden. She stared at him, her mouth open.

She turned to her excited family, who crowded around now, well pleased with her reaction. "Do people live here?" she demanded.

"*You* live here!" someone informed her.

"Yes, and I think we'll take you to your rooms now, Shakira," Dana said quietly, because it was very evident that the princess, still half a boy, half in her former life, had had about as much as she could handle for the moment.

2
Shakira

Shakira's Dream

In the dream they dressed her in flowing robes of unimaginable beauty and delicacy, embroidered with threads and jewels that glowed and shimmered in the soft light of the magical place that was, miraculously, her home. The face that looked back from the mirror as they fussed around her was mysterious and deeply feminine, and the curls that clustered over her head enhanced the delicate bone structure, and the wonder and gratitude she felt burned her eyes.

In the dream, guards in fabulous dress uniform saluted her as she walked through a huge, arched doorway into a hall so bright her eyes hurt. The hall was jammed with magnificently dressed people, who turned to look up and smile with wide-eyed approval as she approached the broad, short flight of marble steps that led from the dais down to the hall.

In the dream her family were there, and in their faces she saw that they were proud of her, and her heart swelled and was filled with sweetness as she looked at them, and felt a part of that larger whole. Felt how she belonged.

Her eyes searched the crowd, in the dream, without her knowing why. As if she were looking for someone. Someone else. Someone not counted among her family.

He *was there then, though she never saw his face. She felt his strength, fierce and protective, felt his warmth, his heat. In the dream, he approached as she came down the steps, her dress rippling and glittering around her as if the sudden soft breeze whispered through the arched openings from the candlelit courtyard just for this moment, for her. He lifted his hand, and she knew he smiled, though she couldn't see his face.*

In the dream she wasn't afraid. She reached out, strong and confident, and placed her hand on his. On her own hand and arm, precious jewels glittered, but no more brightly than the approval in his dark eyes.

Six

RETURN OF LOST PRINCESS
Exclusive Photos of the Boy Princess!

The royal family of Bagestan is celebrating today behind closed doors as they welcome home another princess, this time one who was long believed dead. Informed sources say Princess Shakira was discovered by chance in an Australian refugee detention centre, where she had been living in disguise as a boy ever since the assassination of her entire family by Ghasib's agents fifteen years ago.

Sources say the boy princess arrived at Bagestan's international airport early yesterday, where she was greeted by the Sultan and Sultana and members of the royal family, including Princesses Noor and Jalia. Shakira, who looked tired and malnourished, wept with happiness as the Sultan, her father's cousin, embraced her. The family have asked for privacy while the Princess takes time to recover from her ordeal.

It was Sharif she wanted. In the utter strangeness of her new surroundings, he was her only link between past and future. He alone knew both what she had come from, and what she was moving towards. It was a comfort to think there was someone who knew her, when she no longer knew herself.

But where was he? She had not seen him since her arrival at the palace. The day had overwhelmed her, in spite of the Sultana's best efforts to soften the impact of the new on her wondering mind. There had been no time to be frightened.

Tonight she had taken a bath in enough water to keep a person alive for a month—warm, and scented with perfumed oil, an unimaginable luxury. She had stayed in the water for an hour, hardly believing it could be true.

But when the servant—her personal maid, the Sultana said—pulled the plug and she understood that the water was being allowed to run away after only one use, Shakira had arrived back in the real world with a bone-breaking jolt. Swallowed up in a lush white towelling garment as big as a blanket, she had screamed at the woman, raining curses down on her head for her wanton waste and stupidity. As Shakira feverishly shoved her aside to stuff the plug back in the hole the bewildered maid had run for help.

Six more staff came into the new princess's apartments, rushing and babbling like people waiting for bags of flour to be thrown off the back of a truck. No one could understand her; it was as if she spoke a foreign language.

"Look, Highness," a grey-haired woman kept saying, turning on a tap to let even more water gush wasted down the sink hole, "there is water, there is water now. The rains came! The Sultan sits on the throne and Allah smiles on us."

"Stop doing that!" Shakira had shrieked, by now practically weeping under the combined assault of such terrible waste and not being able to make herself understood.

"The rains came, Princess!" the housekeeper said again.

One of the women, very bravely, had slipped away to the Sultana, and Dana came, bringing instant calm with her presence.

"You are very right, Shakira," she had said, smiling gently. "Someone should have explained to you that waste water from all our bathtubs and sinks goes into a reservoir for use in the palace gardens. I will show you the tanks in the morning."

That had calmed her; it was impossible not to feel gentled by the Sultana's rich, warm voice. Still, Shakira wondered if she would ever get used to the luxury of baths and showers.

She wanted to tell Sharif about that—about how amazing it was to have such an abundance of water. He had followed her trail through so many of the camps. He had seen. He knew.

Now Shakira crept from the too-soft bed—where she had lain sleepless for hours, listening and watching while night birds called, the fountains were stilled and the moon climbed the sky—and slipped barefoot out onto her balcony.

The palace was silent, the sliver of moon reflected in the still, smooth water of the pool. Hidden low amongst the flowers and plants, muted lights glowed at intervals, giving the garden an air of magic; above, from one or two rooms, lamplight showed that the occupants were still awake. One of the lights, like a beacon, glowed from the room Sharif had pointed out earlier as his own. Her heart gave a little kick. It comforted her to know that he, too, was awake, even if she could not talk to him.

Shakira knelt on the cool tiles, her arms resting on the rim of the balcony, her chin on her arms, and watched the tiny crescent of bright moon. Was it really the same moon she had seen from the camp? Or had the world changed, along with her life?

Nothing was certain. In the camps there had been ruthless certainties, harsh and sharp, always reminding her who she was, where she was, that she was alive. *When you are hungry,* she thought, *at least you are certain of that.* Here she could be sure of nothing, not even what was real and what a dream.

A shadow moved across the lamp in Sharif's room. Her nameless yearning attacked her more fiercely. *He* would tell her. He would understand.

She gazed hungrily at the light from the stormy sea of uncertainty, wanting to reach it and be saved. So close, and yet so out of reach. She had seen little of the palace today, only enough to gain the impression of an overwhelming confusion of corridors and doors. Hani had found a secret way out of Burry Hill, but at the thought of finding her way around those corridors Shakira's courage failed her.

She would never find his room if she went searching, and yet she knew exactly where it was. That contradiction was disturbing, underlining the truth that she was in an unknown world. A world where the skills she had learned over a lifetime were suddenly pointless.

And yet—were they? His light beckoned her. The Princess stood and peered over her balcony into the shadowed courtyard, her hands against the warm, breathing marble. The delicately carved surround of each balcony offered a thousand toeholds to the agile.

And a moment later, her bandaged ankle hampering her hardly at all, she was over the balcony and down. As her muscles took her weight she was suffused with a sense of relief: she was not completely lost in this new environment. Her life skills could still be put to good use.

The tile paving of the courtyard was cool and smooth under her bare feet as she crept among the shadows across to the opposite wing. Then, after a moment to get her bearings, she clambered up again, monkey agile, and slipped silently into the moonless gloom of Sharif's balcony.

His door was open on the night. Inside he sat at a large black desk, bent over some papers. Shakira paused for a moment, a smile pulling at her lips as she watched him. He signed a paper and moved it to one side, read another. Then he frowned as he searched for something in a stack of documents.

He was different now—his face was stern and distant in the lamplight—and Shakira shifted nervously. Perhaps she didn't know him after all. Perhaps he would not be glad to see her, as she was to see him.

Sharif tossed down his pen to reach for the gold cigar case lying in the lamp glow. It flicked open, and he drew out one of his small cigars and closed it again. The sound of the click was sharp on the night air.

Suddenly, as if he had sensed her presence, one dark eyebrow went up and his head turned towards the dark balcony. For a moment he frowned into the darkness just beyond the circle of lamp glow, then, as if he had recognized her, his face relaxed. He dropped the thin cigar and the case and held out an imperious hand.

"Come," said Sharif.

She slipped into the light as stealthily as any cat burglar, her eyes huge in the thin little face.

"Can't sleep, little one?"

The tenderness in his voice made her heart leap, and the approval in his eyes was dangerous for the way it melted her defences. But she had been through too much today to be able to resist the melting. She could not be defended now—she could only smile nervously as she moved to his side.

"My bed is too soft," she confided, moving closer to stand against his arm.

"It's been a very exciting day." His dark eyes seemed to see into her. How dangerous to be so known, some Hani part of her cried, but she could not turn away from that tenderly piercing gaze.

"I wish you were my brother," she said, because, for all her linguistic virtuosity with insult, she was awkward expressing any gentler emotion. "He was there, and then they took me away and I never saw him again."

She looked at him with aching yearning, as if he might suddenly discover a lost history of his own that would make this possible.

"We will look for your brother one day soon," he promised.

She smiled against the tears that suddenly burnt her eyes. For so many years she hadn't cried at all, and now, suddenly, when tears were no longer necessary, she couldn't hold them back.

"The only thing that's the same is the moon!" she cried suddenly. "How can all this be real, when it's so different—I used to dream it, you know. I dreamed of people calling me Princess, and loving me. I'm afraid…I'm afraid…"

She could not go on, because of the sobs that came tumbling out of her throat. "I'm afraid," she said again, who had learned never to admit to fear. It was her safety with him that made her weep.

He pushed back his chair and stood. Then he wrapped his arm around her and led her through a doorway to his own bedroom. A thick mat lay on the floor, with cushions and pillows spread around. The sheet had been folded back ready for him, and he bent to lift it for her.

"This is not a dream," he said, with firm reassurance. "When you wake up you will still be here, in the palace, among your family."

Something tight inside her unwound suddenly, for he had understood something about her that she had not understood about herself. And being understood, the thing lost its power.

Shakira yawned as fatigue hit her. Without a word she sank down onto the mat and slipped her feet under the sheet as he drew it up over her.

"This is not so soft," she said, smiling at him. "It is better, isn't it?"

He only smiled, and she yawned again.

"Where will you sleep?" she asked drowsily, tucking her arms around the pillow and giving herself to its soft comfort. "I can sleep on the floor, you know."

"So can I, little one. Don't worry."

"My room is very big," Shakira said, by way of explanation. "I've never been alone in such a big room. This is better, with you here."

"I won't leave you," he promised.

Her hand left the pillow and reached out to him, and he sank down and took it in his. Again he felt the assault of that painful thinness, and his heart clenched.

"I'm sleepy now," she said.

He reached and put out the light, and in the same instant the little hand went trustingly slack in his, and the urchin slept.

"It's a shock, but it's a pretty wonderful one when you get used to it," Noor said, with a warm smile. "Isn't it funny that you were in that camp in Oz all that time, and I was in Sydney, and we didn't know anything about each other's existence? And all the time we were cousins."

Shakira could only smile at this glowing creature who called her cousin. On her other side, Princess Jalia gently took her hand. "It's very satisfying to find another cousin, when that monster was trying to kill us all," she murmured.

Shakira sighed as tendrils of happiness branched in her. The three princess cousins were sitting together by the fountain in the courtyard, in the shade of a large tree, relaxing after Shakira's first Friday evening dinner with all her family.

"You have to be a bridesmaid at our wedding, Shakira! Isn't it lucky—I would have been married already, but it was cancelled at the last minute! You'll be hearing all about that, but not now." Noor laughed and flicked a roguish glance at Jalia, who only shook her head. "Jalia and I are planning a double wedding, and now I think it was fate, because now you can be one of our bridesmaids! We're going to have a *wonderful* time getting you kitted out for it, aren't we, Jay?"

Shakira's panic must have shown in her eyes.

"Don't worry, we've got months!" Jalia hastily reassured her. "Noor and Bari's wedding had to be postponed when Bari's grandfather died suddenly, and we decided to do it together."

"So—first things first! What you need right now is some serious pampering," Noor declared. "Haircut, massage, manicure—you name it, I've got the perfect person to do it."

Shakira was feeling overwhelmed. She licked her lips. "I've never had anything like that," she said nervously.

Noor's smile was warm in her eyes. "That's no problem," she said gently. "There's a first time for everything."

"You'll soon find out that Noor's used to the pampered life," Jalia said. "She slipped into the princess thing like a made-to-measure glove. For you and me, it's more of a shock."

"When I was a…young, my—my stepmother always cut my hair. Then it was the camp barber, or I did it myself. And…I don't know what those other things are," Shakira told them. She glanced uncertainly from Noor to Jalia. She was so much more used to being with men than women. Women were somehow like her memory of her mother—warm, soft, sweet-smelling and a little mysterious. It was hard to believe she could ever be like that.

"I don't really know anything about being a girl," she confessed.

Noor smiled and nodded as if that were a problem you ran into every day. "No worries. We'll teach you."

There was so much to learn, so much she had missed. When they took her through the palace, telling her about the portraits, the beautiful miniatures, the great bronze trays that formed part of the artistic treasure of the nation and the family she was part of, she was equal parts enthralled by the stories and dismayed that she knew so little of her history.

"This is your ancestor Akram," Sharif said one day, stopping in front of a haunting portrait of a man wearing an intri-

cately sculpted crown. "He fought a war with the great World
Burner, Ahmad Shah, and the Emperor was so impressed with
his bravery and strategy that, although the empire's superior
numbers meant Akram would inevitably be crushed, he offered Akram a truce. As long as Ahmad Shah lived, they were
allies, and that is why Bagestan was never conquered by the
Moghuls. It must have been his blood in your veins, Princess,
that made you so dauntless in adversity."

Shakira gazed at the stern, noble face. "He is like you," she
said softly, for what she saw was not eyes and mouth, but the
heroic humanity of the portrait.

She was enchanted by Sharif's stories, thrilled by them. Although many in her family took part in this area of her education, the stories he chose to tell her somehow seemed to
connect to her own experience. Sharif's retelling of history
made her feel proud not merely of her brave ancestors, but of
herself. As if, in surviving the life she had, Shakira had been
following in their footsteps. He made her feel that she had always been a princess.

"This is the great Suhayr, your ancestress, who ruled Bagestan
after her husband died, while her son was too young to rule.
When she was threatened by a great army, she sent a message
to the King. 'Why do you invade my country, at such cost to your
reputation? For if you defeat me, they will say only that you have
defeated a woman. But if Allah should grant me the victory, they
will say that you have been defeated by a woman.' And he was
struck by the truth of her argument, and withdrew his army."

She loved listening to him, and in giving her her lost past,
he also gave her her lost self—as an artist restores a work of
art, painstakingly filling in the blank areas of the pattern.

The way he had given her her name.

At night, still, when she couldn't sleep, she often crept across
to his room, clambering up the balcony to appear at his window with dark questing eyes, never quite sure of her welcome.
Sometimes, if he were still at his desk, she would sit and

watch as he worked, drinking tea and munching the burnt sugar medallions that a servant had left warming for him. If it was late, he would put her straight to bed, and sit beside her as she fell asleep.

The times she liked best were the nights when he tossed down his pen and they spread cushions on the balcony and he sat with her there, watching moonlight turn the garden into a place even more magical than it was by day. He told her stories from fairy tale and from history, and she told him stories of her past. England, and the camps, and the hazy, happy time before, with her family.

She told him most often of her brother, dreaming that Mazin was still alive, and how it would be when they met again at last.

There was one story she never told him. It came to her tongue many times, but Shakira bit it back. It was a horror story, from the camps, but however many stirring adventures Sharif described to her from her family's past, this was a part of her that could never be told.

Seven

*A*llahu akbaar…. Allahu akbaar….

Shakira awoke in the first grey of dawn, to the sound of the muezzin.

God is great.

She sat up with a start, gazing around in the gloom. Where was she? Why was she alone in such a big tent? And why was the tent so clean? Its sides fell in gauzy white folds all around the space where she lay. That, too, was covered in clean, white cloths. Behind her were fluffy cushions and pillows, and room enough for a dozen others to sleep. But where were they?

Come to prayer.

It was a sound from her childhood, but unfamiliar now. Had she died? Was this heaven?

It must be. Everything so clean and white, and with so much space all to herself—she was in heaven. How strange that she didn't remember her death!

Slowly memory began to return—first, that she no longer slept under a tent, but in a small, hot room in Burry Hill Detention Centre. Then she had a vision of Sharif Azad al Dauleh, and then, in a sudden rush, she remembered everything.

The palace. She was in her room—her *rooms,* for the apartment she had been given was large. She had been home, with her true family, for nearly three weeks.

Come to prayer. In the camps there had been no muezzin, and whether she slept like the dead, as she had last night, or tossed for hours wondering at the silence and the luxury that surrounded her, or, most happily, fell asleep on the cushions on Sharif's balcony, the call awakened her in the morning.

The voice reminded her of a time long past, when, at the door of her father's study, she would see him at prayer, and know that all was right with her world because her father talked to God. She could almost hear the low murmur of his voice now.

Bismillah arrahman arraheem....

Shakira slipped to the edge of the bed, whose firm softness she was at last getting used to, and reached her feet down to the still astonishing silkiness of the beautiful white carpet. In the gloom the pattern of delicate arabesques and guls in a palette of greens seemed like mystical symbols rising from a white sea.

The sky outside was slowly paling to reveal the room. The Sultana had somehow understood, and the newfound princess had been given a bedroom decorated in pure white. To be so clean! It was like a dream. No wonder she had imagined she was waking in heaven.

In the bathroom she brushed her teeth, then ritually washed her face and hands and feet, still sparing with the water, and remembering her first, luxurious bath in this room. In the bedroom again she stepped over to the prayer rug lying in one corner and, with gratitude deep in her heart, softly began the recital of the dawn prayer, as she had heard her father do so long ago.

In the name of God, the Compassionate, the Merciful...

Afterwards, she stepped out onto the balcony overlooking the courtyard and the reflecting pool. As always, her heart lifted at the harmony of so much natural and man-made beauty. The fountains were silent at this hour, the water flat and smooth, with the early light glinting from the still surface. The magnificent domed balcony where generations of monarchs had taken their leisure was perfectly repeated in the mirror of the water.

On the other side of the court lay Sharif's apartment, and as always at this hour, his light was already on: the Cup Companions of the Sultan worked hard and long in the great task of helping him rebuild the country.

Shakira smiled and leaned on the balustrade, waiting for him to appear, as he did every morning, to greet her.

A gardener with a rake walked by below, yawning. Lights were coming from a few ground-floor windows, for many of the palace staff were already settling to their work, starting early while it was still cool, in order to rest in the heat of the day.

What a difference from life in Burry Hill, where no one had anything productive to do! There had been no sense of purpose in the camps, no buzz of useful activity as she sensed here, not only in the palace, but everywhere in the country.

Shakira had eagerly asked the Sultana what work she would be assigned to, but Dana said only, "For now, you have plenty to do just recovering, and getting used to things, and getting to know your family."

And in truth, that was enough. As well as learning to find her way about the palace and getting to know the various members of her family, past and present, she had been caught up in a whirlwind of pampering, discovery and laughter as the three cousins undertook what Noor had dubbed The Princess Makeover Project.

When she passed a mirror now Shakira only blinked at herself. Her hair was only a half inch of curl, wrapped around her skull like a cap. Even to make her a boy they had never cut her hair so short.

"The hair's too damaged to recover. Best to take it all off," Noor's hairdresser had insisted. At first Shakira had looked even more starved, though everyone pretended she didn't. But now they didn't have to pretend so hard—Shakira was already putting flesh between skin and bone.

Her skin glowed with sweet-smelling creams and oils, too. Shakira lifted her arm and sniffed the still faintly lingering scent. How strange to have a perfumed cream! They had asked her which cream she wanted, and she had chosen the pink one that smelled of roses, and thought how strange it was that she should smell like the memory of her mother.

She wore clean clothes every day. That seemed a miracle, too—the closets and cupboards so full of clean new clothes, the maid holding things up for her to say what she wanted. She wore white most of the time because she couldn't get over the magic of whiteness. Her sandals were white, too, the softest leather she had ever touched. Even the pyjamas she wore now in the fresh morning air, watching as the palace awoke, waiting for Sharif to appear, were white.

Sharif hadn't flinched when he saw her almost-bald head. His face had been the same as always. As if…she searched for it…as if he had always seen what was inside anyway, and the outside didn't matter.

She wiggled her almost-healed ankle, and was reminded of that first meeting, on the road. That first sight of him, so tall and noble, defending her from the trucker…she had felt hungry for something she couldn't name. The right to trust someone, perhaps. The longing had made her feel weak, and that was dangerous.

But in the end she had trusted him. And her life had…

"Princess!"

She wouldn't have heard the whisper if she hadn't had every sense alert. Shakira leaned over and peered into the gloom of his balcony.

"Look down!"

A shadowed figure was standing below in the courtyard, but even without the voice she would have known who it was.

"Sharif!"

"Good morning," he called softly. "Did you sleep well?"

"Yes. The muezzin woke me. What are you doing down there? Wait!"

She leapt up onto the balcony wall and, clinging to the arabesques sculpted into the stone face, went over and down with the fearless aplomb of a monkey.

"Dammit, Princess!" Sharif complained, watching helplessly as she clambered down to the balcony below, then over that and down again, her legs kicking the air for a moment until they found the tiled pillar. She clung to that with practised ease and slid down till she was standing beside him, barefoot and rumpled.

"Good morning, Hani," he remarked dryly, and she tilted her head back and laughed her gamin laugh at his apt use of the name. Sharif always knew.

"This is nice, to walk in the garden before it is light," she said, as they turned and followed in the wake of the sleepy gardener. A leaf fell on the pool, sending ripples through the perfectly reflected image of the columns and dome of the *talar*. The tiles were cool underfoot, but the breeze carried the scent of the day's heat to come. Shakira bent and picked up a fallen blossom that was still fresh, and touched its tender leaves with wondering hands.

She lifted it to her face, finding joy in the silkiness and the scent.

"Smell," she commanded him softly; and he bent his face to it, and the rose was between his mouth and her palm like a kiss.

When he straightened again, neither knew whether a moment had passed, or a lifetime.

"Princess, I came to say goodbye," Sharif began.

He saw it hit her, a lightning bolt cracking through her, and he cursed himself for his stupid clumsiness. Words had a different meaning for this child. When would he learn that?

The big dark eyes, still circled with hollows of deprivation, fixed his face in incredulous denial.

"*Goodbye?* Are you leaving?" she cried. She did not pronounce the word, but he could hear it. *Me.*

"Only for a week or two, probably," he supplied hastily. "But it might be longer. I can't be sure."

She scarcely seemed to hear. *"Why?"*

Should he have foreseen this? What had made him underestimate his impact on her life so grossly? He remembered the way she had pronounced that word *family.* Remembered her soul-deep joy. Now she was surrounded with family, and yet...

He should have known. If he, whose heart was rarely touched by feelings of deep connection with another human creature, felt that the tendrils of this child's essence had somehow reached into the deepest parts of his self, was it really so hard to understand that she, too, felt a bond?

"Why?" she cried again.

He hesitated. They had decided against telling her, but now—what was best?

"It's—I must go, Princess," he said at last. "The Sultan has given me an assignment...to—"

"Tell him no! Why does it have to be you?"

"Princess, when the Sultan requests a thing, it is *hearing and obeying,*" he said awkwardly.

"You can't go!" she said, fiercely angry, because it would be weakness to be hurt, weakness to plead.

Sharif pressed his lips together, more and more furious with himself. There were a dozen better ways he could have handled this.

"You are with your family now, Shakira. You won't miss me as much as you—"

"Don't—" she began fiercely, and then, abruptly, her feelings shut down. Miss him? Why should she miss him? She had her family, and even if she hadn't, she didn't need anyone! She could survive, she always had.

His heart protested as he watched her face close against him. Her eyes lost all expression. She shrugged her thin shoulders up around her ears and forgot to lower them.

"I don't care if you go." Her lively voice was dead, flat and dismissive. "I don't need you. I have my family now," she said, as if he hadn't just said the same thing.

"Shakira, we weren't going to tell you why I'm going, but I think it's best if I do. The Sultan—"

"I don't care!" It was true. Her heart had performed the old familiar function, though she was hardly aware of it, shutting its gates against the pain of loss. "Anyway, I won't miss you, because my grandmother is coming to see me today," she told him haughtily, hardly remembering how she had treasured up this joy to share with him. And now, instead of a shared joy, it was armour against him.

Something in him urged him to break down the walls she had suddenly erected, but he would not obey the urge. He had to go, and she would forgive him when she learned the reason. But it was better if she did not know now.

And it was true enough—she had her family.

"Ah," he said, smiling a little. "So today you meet the great Suhaila? That is excellent news."

"Yes!" she cried, still angry. "She's a famous singer, Sharif! So you see I don't care if you won't be here, because I will be talking with my grandmother!"

She tossed something down, turned and ran back up the tiled path. At the pillar beneath her own balcony, she leapt up and clung, and with hands, knees and feet, swarmed up till her fingers found a better hold in the sculpted stone. Then, lightly, agilely, without a backward glance, she went up and over the wall and was gone.

He bent to pick up the discarded flower at his feet. Its hurt perfume scented the air strongly now: its heart had been crushed by those thin, agile fingers.

Eight

Suhaila was a tiny, vivid woman, dressed in the most gorgeous silks, her expressive hands and arms crusted with a rich display of jewels and the gold bracelets Shakira remembered, her long braided hair a rebellious black, and her black eyes bright with humour, mischief, wisdom and defiance.

"Ah, you are like me," she said to Shakira. "The eyes, of course—there you are like Safa. But you are small and thin, like me, and you have no breasts. And your chin—" she put out a firm hand to stroke her granddaughter's cheek "—these things you have from me. Your breasts will grow now that you are eating, but you will always be a small woman. And you are a fighter, one sees that in your face. I was a fighter, too. Beware, Granddaughter, because it doesn't always lead to happiness. How old are you?"

"I—twenty-one, I think." Her birth date had been lost long ago in the camps, but she had learned her real statistics from the records in the Sultan's dossier.

"Mahlouf was a fool to go back to Bagestan when he did,"

the old woman said. "I told him so, but if there is any way to stop a young man being a fool, I never learned it. Even if he had not been Prince Safa's son, the fact that his mother was abroad recording songs of the resistance would have put him in danger."

Shakira smiled shyly, entranced by her grandmother's fire and strength. "They played *Aina al Warda* for me," she said. *Where is the Rose?* Suhaila's voice asked so urgently, so plaintively, that Shakira, in company with many other Bagestanis, wept every time she heard it. "It's very beautiful. The Sultan said the whole resistance movement was fired by the way you sang that song."

In fact, she loved her grandmother's singing so much that she had played little else since learning how to work the CD player in her sitting room.

Suhaila laughed, but she was clearly pleased. *"Mash'Allah!* And did you inherit my voice?" asked "Bagestan's Nightingale."

"I don't know. I wasn't allowed to sing."

The old woman fixed her with a thoughtful look, then nodded. "Ghasib had his spies looking for you, of course, and he knew whose granddaughter you were. If a child in Arif Bahrami's family had been heard to have a voice…"

Shakira blinked, remembering a day when the family had been visiting a public garden. It had been a beautiful day, cool after an overnight rain, and the roses had been in bloom. Hani had felt his heart lighten, not knowing why, but the next moment a blow from his stepmother on the back of his head had shocked him out of whatever dream he had inhabited.

Don't sing! she had hissed at him.

"Is that why?" Shakira asked now. It had seemed so unreasonable that Hani's heart had nearly burst with the injustice. One of the many incomprehensible embargoes on the child's behaviour. Like being a boy instead of a girl.

Her grandmother lifted her hands, and a hundred gold bracelets tinkled on her arms, just as they had in memory.

"What other reason? Bahrami was a great loyalist. He knew how far Ghasib's paranoia extended."

With a shock of shifting images, Shakira's past reconfigured itself. "I thought it was because she hated me," she murmured. "She always seemed so angry."

"Perhaps she was always afraid." Suhaila nodded. "Well, then, perhaps you have a voice. One day we will see. Other things are more important right now."

"Grandmother—" How her heart beat with the word! "Grandmother, will you tell me about you and my grandfather? And my father and mother? Will you tell me everything?"

The great singer laughed, and stroked her cheek again. "That is why I am here, child." She settled herself on the divan, amongst an array of fat cushions, as if she were a Sultan herself. "Today I will tell you about your handsome grandfather, Prince Safa. Sit there."

She was so regal it would have been impossible to disobey, but of course Shakira had no such thought anyway. With stars in her eyes she sank down at her grandmother's knee.

"My father, your great-grandfather, was a very educated and forward-looking man, a brother of a Johari tribal chief. One of his brothers was Cup Companion to the Crown Prince.

"When I was a girl there was war in Europe, and the armies of the West invaded countries around Bagestan, to keep the oil for themselves. My father said that it was a warning for the future. No one could predict with certainty what would happen, except that the world was changing, and that his daughters as well as his sons must be educated for a profession. *Mash'Allah* I was blessed with the voice of a *bulbul,* and my father gave his permission for me to sing in public, and to have a career. Many in the family thought this shocking, as if I had become a woman of the streets, but my father never failed me. He said that only fools buried their heads.

"I was already becoming a well-known singer when Prince Safa came to one of my concerts. He was a wild young man, a wealthy prince who owned racehorses and drove a sports car. And he dated beautiful women, foreign actresses and a European princess.

"But when he saw me he fell in love. He said he had never loved in his life before, and I believed him, because I, too, had fallen in love. He was so generous, and such a handsome man! Prince Safa was commander of one of his father's horse regiments, though he did not take his duties seriously, and the uniform was the most becoming of the whole army. Oh, he was very dashing, with a black moustache and black eyes that looked straight to the heart of a woman! Anyone who saw him mounted on that devil of a black horse lost her heart."

Shakira sighed and, led by her grandmother's voice, lost herself in imagining.

"Well, we were in love, but although I sang in public I was nevertheless a member of an important family. And I was very closely chaperoned. Only marriage was possible between us, but Safa knew that the Sultan would forbid it. He wanted Safa to marry his cousin. So, young and foolish, we married privately.

"Safa's grandfather was an old man, in the last years of his reign then—Hafzuddin was still Crown Prince—and he was outraged when Safa took me to the palace and introduced me as his wife.

"He said that I must give up my public singing at once and live within the harem like his own wives. But I was young, and full of new ideas about women's freedom, and a fire-brand—and I had never been spoken to by my father in the way the Sultan spoke to me. I, too, was angry." The old woman smiled. "And I had just been offered a contract for a tour of Bagestan, Parvan, Barakat, Kaljukistan, and Joharistan. It was an important step in my career, and I was determined to go.

"We fought it out, the old man and I, and everyone was horrified that I dared to speak to the Sultan in such a way, that I defied him so openly.

"Safa did not confront his grandfather with me. All his

training was against such a thing. He remained silent. He wanted me to give in, to sing only in the palace for the rest of my life. *Sing to me,* he said. *I will be your concert hall. I will love you enough for a hundred thousand others.*

"But I could not. And so—it was a very short-lived thing, our marriage. I left the palace in the car that took me on the first stage of my tour. Safa would not come with me. At his grandfather's insistence, he divorced me as I left. I can hear his voice now. *I divorce thee.* Later he said that he had only said it to bring me to my senses. But I was headstrong! If he could divorce me…so be it! And so I went."

It had all happened nearly a half century before, but it was closer to Shakira's heart than her own breath.

"Oh, Grandmother!" she whispered sadly.

"Perhaps I should have considered longer. But I was young and beautiful and with a rare voice, and they told me I could ask for the world and get it. You, Granddaughter, have learned the value of family and love in one way, through having none. I had everything—a close, loving family, a caring father—and their love had never made any demands. Now a prince was in love with me and I thought that his love asked too high a price. It *was* too high, but perhaps I should have paid it." She sighed heavily, then turned and stroked Shakira's cheek, her damp eyes smiling. "But it is strange, is it not?—whatever I had chosen then, you and I would probably still be sitting here today. You see, Granddaughter, how our small personal choices may mean nothing when politics and war enter our lives."

"What happened then?"

"On the tour I learned that I was pregnant. Our marriage had been kept secret, and apart from our families, only a few very close friends knew. The public would have been unforgiving even if they had known I was married and had been divorced for the sake of my career. If they imagined that I had taken a lover and become pregnant outside marriage, my career would be ruined overnight.

"I would have gone back, to try again with Safa, because I missed him so much more than I had imagined, and anyway, a child changes everything. But the tour was enormously popular. My manager did not want me to give up in the middle. He offered to marry me, to pretend the child was his own. He was older than I was, much older. I didn't know it then, but Majdi, too, loved me. In his way.

"I sent a message to the palace, to Safa, telling him the position. I said I would wait two weeks for his answer, and I told Majdi that if Safa did not come in two weeks, I would marry him.

"Safa did not come. He did not send a message. No answer of any kind. Even at the last moment I was looking down the street, hoping for a car, a horse...I knew then that Safa had not really loved me, and I had made the right choice. I married Majdi and named my son Mahlouf. That is your father. I wrote to Safa, a very bitter letter, to tell him that his son had the al Jawadi eyes, even if not the name.

"He came to see us then. He was in a terrible rage. He had never received my message. Majdi had destroyed my letter and only pretended to send it."

"Oh!" Shakira's eyes were burning, her throat tight. "What happened? You couldn't..."

The old woman shook her head. "It was too late then. There was no way back. I was another man's wife. There would have been a terrible scandal if I had divorced Majdi to marry Prince Safa. And with a child—who would have believed that we had been married before? People would have said that the prince had been my lover and my husband had divorced me because my child was not his own—it would have been an impossible position.

"We were never together again, but we loved each other till the end," said Suhaila, and the expressive dark eyes were suddenly liquid with tears. "The day that Safa was assassinated, my heart was pierced with the same bullet."

Nine

FIRST PUBLIC APPEARANCE OF
LOST PRINCESS

Princess Shakira appeared in public for the first time yesterday, on the balcony of the Jawad Palace, with the Sultan and other members of her family, when a spontaneous demonstration took place in Shah Jawad Square.

The crowd, which some estimates put at 100,000, had gathered in response to persistent rumours that the popular singer Suha was staying at the palace. They were rewarded after several hours by the appearance of the singer, whom Bagestanis of all walks cherish for her stirring recordings of anti-Ghasib songs during the long exile.

The crowd cheered itself hoarse when the singer was joined by the Sultan and Sultana and other members of the family. A boyish figure thought to be Princess Shakira was spotted standing beside the Sultana.

A microphone was eventually rigged up and the crowd got what it wanted at last: with the Sultan at her side, the great Suha sang *Aina al Warda,* the signature song of the Bagestani resistance movement. Bagestanis are always an emotional people, but this time they outdid themselves, shouting and cheering and sobbing on each other's shoulders, and refusing to disperse until the old singer had repeated the song three times.

The central bazaar of Medinat al Bostan was a nest of alleyways behind the main square, not far from the great Shah Jawad Mosque, and as he walked along its central passage, Sharif Azad al Dauleh could see, through the arch at the top, the sun glowing from the magnificent golden dome and the high, exquisitely fashioned minarets that surrounded it.

All around him women and shopkeepers were haggling over price and quality, as they had done in this spot for probably thousands of years. The bazaar was a bustle of humanity, as usual on Thursday afternoon, when all the world came out to shop in preparation for Juma. Since the restoration of the mosque as a place of worship, Fridays in the capital had an air of jubilation. Under Ghasib the ancient twelfth-century mosque had been converted into a museum, and worship had been displaced to a small nearby mosque with none of the architectural magnificence that had made the Shah Jawad Mosque a World Heritage Site.

No longer. Tourists were still allowed to visit the holy place, but not on Friday at the noon prayer. Then it was filled to overflowing with worshippers from all over the city who came to worship in Bagestan's holiest shrine.

He had been absent a month. He always missed the city, the most beautiful city in the world. Coming to the palace now by way of the bazaar was his manner of greeting his old friend. The smell that was a mixture of spices, sugar, perfume, ancient stone, and incense was profoundly evocative, and the sight of the golden-domed mosque through the archway was one of his earliest childhood memories.

He was tired, and very glad to be back, though he had failed completely in the central mission that had taken him away.

He would be seeing Princess Shakira again. He had thought about her often during his absence, wondering what was happening in her life, her heart, what transitions were taking place. Although she had a huge family, in a curious way he felt responsible for her. He had plucked her from the hell of an empty life, a life without a future, and had taken her to her rightful home. It was not an everyday experience, he told himself, and no wonder if he felt an ongoing interest in the outcome, even if Shakira herself had by now forgotten his part in the proceedings entirely.

What kind of woman had she become?

Vibrant and honest, he was sure. He remembered her way of clambering up and down balconies and wondered if she had turned palace protocol upside down with her engaging, direct ways.

Probably she would prove to be a beautiful woman, in the end. Her grandmother's beauty had captured a prince, after all, and she was still a beauty nearly fifty years later. And Rabia, her great-grandmother, if the portrait in the Sultan's Antechamber didn't lie, had been another.

Not that she needed her forebears' beauty. Her face had been with him constantly. She was haunting, even when she had been starved to the bone.

The past month must have made a big difference, and he was both sorry to have missed the transition and deeply interested to see what kind of woman the Princess was making of herself.

Ahead of him, suddenly, a street urchin came milling out of a vegetable stall, the proprietor shouting and clutching at his grubby kaftan. The boy, cursing and kicking, grabbed a basket as he struggled. A cascade of purple-black aubergines spilled down, bouncing and rolling across the passage as shoppers danced out of the way.

"Let me go, camel-stuffer!"

At the sound of the voice, Sharif's eyebrows shot up, and he turned to watch the fracas with frowning interest.

A box of fat tomatoes went over next. Shoppers in the narrow alley created a small jam as they stopped to watch, or tried to gather the tumbling fruit. After a short struggle, Hani slipped out of the shopkeeper's hold and dived into the little crowd. Twisting like a fish among reeds, he was through and gone in a moment.

On Friday evenings the Sultan and Sultana regularly hosted a family meal in their apartments, to which family members and Cup Companions had a standing invitation.

Today, the traditional *sofreh* was spread on the ground in the private courtyard. The cloth was covered with a tantalizing variety of food, including huge platters heaped with flavoured rice. Nearby the tumbling fountain cooled the air.

It was a smaller group than usual: the Sultan and several of his Cup Companions were away consulting with tribal leaders. Shakira saw Sharif the moment he stepped out of the shaded cloister to stride across the grass towards the picnic, and her heart leapt straight for her throat.

"Sharif!" she cried, and all the lies she had told herself about not caring were burnt up by the bright flame of her joy at seeing him again. She watched every step of his approach, her eyes getting bigger and darker with every footfall, revealing an unconscious longing that drew him like a net.

"Hello, Princess," he said quietly, a smile drawing up the corners of his mouth as he looked at her. She had gained weight, and her head had lost the skull-like look. The high cheekbones and square jaw were now covered with healthy flesh, and her chin was softly rounded. Her cheeks, he saw, would always be hollow, giving her face a regal elegance. The black smudges had gone from under her eyes. Her expertly cut hair had grown, and dark curls clustered over her head and neck, revealing a small widow's peak and well-shaped ears. Now for the first time the adult Shakira would have been recognizable in that childhood photograph.

She was wearing white, against which her mocha skin gave off a deeply attractive warmth. She wore no makeup, no jewellery. She seemed still halfway between the boy she had been and the woman she would be. But she had travelled far enough along the path for him to know that he was right: she was going to be a beautiful woman. A stunningly individual beauty, too, he thought.

"It's been a good month, I see."

She gazed up, smiling with the pleasure of seeing approval in his eyes. He was very tall, standing over her. He wore a black kaftan that made his eyes very dark, with a green keffiyeh tossed back over his shoulders. Wind caught the robe suddenly, pressing against him, but he stood easily against it, and it seemed to her that his strength would be equal to anything.

"You said a week, but you never came back," she said, in her direct way, as he sat beside her.

"I had much more troublesome work than we had imagined, Princess. I'm sorry." He took a piece of hot *naan* bread from the nearest basket.

Shakira sighed.

"I thought—I thought—sometimes I thought you were dead."

The remembered pain burned in her eyes. Sharif was shaken to his roots. He tossed down the bread and gripped her wrist.

"*Ya Allah,* why didn't you ask the Sultan?" he said, though his impatience was directed at himself. He might have guessed this.

"I don't know," she murmured. She didn't know how to explain the misery of trying not to miss him, of thinking him dead because it was easier than thinking he had just gone away.

He knew why. Because she was too used to loss to challenge it. Either he was dead or he didn't care about her, and life goes on. He shook his head with remorse. He knew her better than anyone, he was suddenly very sure of that, and he should have been more careful. He had thought he would become unimportant in her life, but he should have known that one more loss would touch that wounded place in her. He should have known that, by his actions in lifting her so abruptly from her former life, he had made himself her rudder in the unknown sea he had brought her to. He should have respected that.

He was suddenly filled with regret that he had not been here to be that rudder.

"Was it important, the reason that took you away?" she asked.

"Very important," he said. "I had more than one job to do, but one of them was…"

He paused. She gazed at him.

"I was searching for your brother, Princess."

Shakira's eyes went wide and dark at a stroke.

"I'm very sorry to have to tell you that I found nothing. Not one lead."

"You—oh, Sharif, you were looking for my brother? Did the Sul—did Ash ask you to do it?"

"I asked for the task. I thought it was very important to you—and I seemed to be the best person for the job. I wish I had been successful, Shakira. But it is very possible that not all avenues have been exhausted yet."

"Nothing? You found nothing?" she said with a desperate appeal that tore his heart to ribbons.

"I'm more sorry than I can say, Princess."

Her eyes burned with tears. "I wish you had told me, that day you left."

"Yes." He didn't remind her that she had spurned his attempt at explanation. "We thought you might think too much about it, if you knew. Your first priority was to settle here."

But she was too honest to accept this glossing over of the truth. "Yes, but you were going to tell me, and I wouldn't listen. I was so angry, Sharif! But afterwards…"

She smiled up into his eyes, and he felt his heart give an involuntary kick. Yes, she was going to be a very beautiful woman.

"I'm glad you're home again," she confided, with a complete lack of feminine guile.

They sat silent for a long moment, and then he mentioned Suhaila.

"My grandmother! Oh, yes!" Shakira said quickly. "She is living in the palace now." She looked around. "She is there, beside Dana."

He obediently looked. Her grandmother and the Sultana were both dressed gorgeously, Dana in turquoise and purple, Suha in red and gold, and Shakira was suddenly conscious of her own very plain *shalwar kamees,* all white with only a little embroidery around the neck and sleeves. For the first time she wondered what it would be like to dress in something really beautiful. Something feminine. She wondered what Sharif would think if she did.

"I am sure that makes you very happy."

"Yes," she said softly. "Everybody loves her. Did you hear? People learned that Suha was here, and they started crowding into the square, shouting her name and demanding to see her. There were thousands of people, and they were shouting for the Sultan, too. Finally we all went out onto the balcony, and Grandmother sang *Aina al Warda.* She changed the last line. Instead of *where is the Rose* she sang, *here is the Rose*." Shakira closed her eyes, remembering the moment. "It was so exciting! The crowd was cheering and crying. Did you see it? I thought about you. I wondered if you were there."

He suddenly realized that what had softened the intense little face was the wiping away of some of the cynicism that had once protected her. He was swept with a feeling of gratitude that it should be so, that her innocence could be restored like this. Gratitude that was closer to joy than anything he had experienced for a long time. Joy—and yet, he realized abruptly, his eyes were burning with unshed tears.

"I was many miles away, but I watched it on television."

"Did you? We watched it, too, afterwards. No one knew the TV people were there till we saw it on the news. Did you see me?" she asked with naive pleasure. "I was standing beside Dana."

Sharif looked at her gravely. "Yes, I saw you. We all saw you."

"That was another strange thing, to see myself like that," she confided. "Until you showed me that photograph, I'd never seen even a picture of myself. Well, except on my camp documents," she amended.

He looked at her for a long moment, considering, then spoke softly, for her ears alone.

"Millions of other people saw you, too, Princess. You will have to be on your guard now."

Her eyes widened with shock, surprise, disbelief. She shifted, uncomfortable under his gaze without knowing why. What was he trying to say? He couldn't *know*. Nobody knew.

"Be careful, Princess."

Neither of them noticed the approach of Suhaila and the Sultana until both women were sitting down beside them.

"Someone who insists on meeting you instantly, Sharif," Dana said with a smile. "Suhaila, this is Sharif ibn Bassam Azad al Dauleh, who found and rescued Shakira. And I'm sure you know, Sharif, that Bagestan's Nightingale is Shakira's grandmother."

The wonderful eyes, still young and vital in the lined face, were wet with tears as the great singer took Sharif's hand in both of hers and thanked him for what he had done.

"Allah must have willed it so, and I thank Him every night that Ashraf chose you for the job, for I don't see how anyone else could have succeeded. An impossible labour! But you did it."

Sharif clasped a fist to his breast.

"Shakira talks about you, you know—'He told me my name,' she says. What gift could one human being give another better than her history, her family, her true self, all in one lost word? You gave my granddaughter her life. And you also gave me…the most precious thing anyone has ever given me." She put her hand on Shakira's cheek, and stroked it lovingly, so that Shakira's heart nearly burst. "You gave me back my lost life. The love I threw aside has been returned to me."

Sharif placed his fist on his heart and bowed.

Suddenly the entire family seemed to realize who had come among them at last, and they all got to their feet, and moved down to where the others sat, and surrounded him, calling their approval and gratitude.

"How did you manage it, Excellency? Especially when she really only looks like Ash when she's in her imp mode!"

"Or when she's angry. How did you get her to lose her temper, Sharif?" someone asked in dry humour, because Shakira was never slow to say what she meant.

Sharif only laughed.

"The palace hasn't been the same since she arrived! I don't know how we got along without her before," Dana said. "We're all very much in your debt."

There was a chorus of agreement. Shakira sat listening, her heart swelling with this unfamiliar happiness. In all her life before, no one had said so many wonderful things about her. She hadn't felt so loved since those distant memories of her mother and father.

And it was somehow even more satisfying because Sharif was there, sharing it with her. He had brought her to this place, and she was glad that he knew she was loved.

* * *

"Every month?" Shakira cried in shock. "Every month for three days? Are you *sure?*"

Noor smiled at her in the mirror. "You really didn't know? You never had a period before?"

With the resilience of youth, Shakira had recovered quickly, and she felt, and knew she looked, a hundred times healthier. But no one had thought to warn her that with a return to health her delayed puberty would kick in.

"I remember once bleeding when I was about—thirteen, I think. I thought it was a…punishment."

Noor frowned. "A punishment for what?"

Shakira looked away. "I thought I was going to die. But it never came back and I just…forgot about it."

"Thought you were going to *die?*" Noor repeated in horror.

"When people bleed from the inside they usually die," Shakira said matter-of-factly. "It means internal injuries."

"But—didn't you ask anyone about it?"

Shakira only shrugged.

Of course she had known that women had periods, but she had simply never considered that information relative to herself. No woman had discussed it in her presence because she had been a boy, and what she had learned from the men had been a kind of masculine paranoia. Women who were bleeding were dangerously moody and couldn't be touched sexually. Women lied about bleeding when they weren't, to punish their husbands and avoid sex. Women who had stopped bleeding were going to bring another child into a life of misery.

It wasn't something you'd go halfway to meet.

"I just never made the connection till now. I guess I would have, if the bleeding had continued, but it didn't."

"Probably because you were half starved. Your body couldn't afford the luxury. I've heard it happens with anorexics, and I guess effectively, you were one. Now that you're getting proper nutrition, your body is starting to function properly. That's *so* good, Shakira, because if it never happened, you know, you wouldn't be able to have babies."

Babies. Shakira stood staring into her own eyes in the mirror. Was it possible? Would she—*could* she have babies one day? Who would be their father?

Ten

She stopped in front of a sweets stall, to watch with a child's fascination as a woman arranged tiny squares of a confection on a tray. As Sharif watched, the sweets-maker smiled at the urchin in front of her, and offered one of the bright lime squares on the end of her spatula.

Shakira accepted the sugared morsel with a smile as wide as if she *had* been the hungry urchin the woman thought her, and popped it into her mouth. Then, with an abruptness that caught him off guard, she turned her head and looked straight at him. Sharif stiffened and dropped his attention to the antique silver lamp on the stall beside him. Shakira chewed the morsel and swallowed, thanked the woman very politely, turned and continued on her way.

She hadn't recognized him, God be thanked. After a moment he took up the trail again, at a safer distance. Ahead, she turned into the main section of the bazaar, and he walked a little faster, for it would be easy to lose her there.

The alley they had been in debouched into the main street

of the bazaar near the arched entrance that framed the mosque. The sun on the golden dome was blinding, seen from the shadowed bazaar, and he stood for a moment frowningly trying to discover which way she had gone.

"Are you following me?" demanded a voice at his elbow. Sharif shook his head ruefully. She hadn't gone anywhere. Oldest trick in the book, and he should have known Hani was wily enough for anything.

He looked down at her. He was now at his leisure to appreciate the artistic smudges of dirt on her face; and the grubby white djellaba and crocheted multi-coloured cap were a neat touch, for it was an outfit no different than what most of the bazaar beggar children wore.

"Hello, Hani," he said.

She caught her breath, then laughed a little. "You are always giving me my name!"

Even so, if anyone looked closely, she could no longer seriously pass for a boy. Her face had filled out, and was softer and more rounded. Her mouth had relaxed into a more feminine fullness. The loose kaftan did not completely disguise the new small curve of breasts. And the curls clustering all around the rim of the cap were too neat, too glossy...too female. With her big dark eyes and wide mouth, she looked like a picture book Aladdin, smudged cheeks and all.

He stood gazing down at her for a long moment of silence. He was aware of a faint breeze. It disturbed the dark curl that fell over the centre of her brow.

"Is it your name?" he challenged softly.

She flung her head up and stared into his eyes with a look so defiantly female that he wanted to shake her. How did she imagine she was safe in this ridiculous boy's disguise?

"Sometimes."

"Only sometimes?"

Before, he had always laughed whenever she had reverted to Hani behaviour. She had felt that Sharif alone understood.

She responded to his challenge now in Hani fashion, with a sudden descent into aggression.

"Why are you following me? What business is it of yours what I do?"

"It's someone's business to keep you out of trouble," he told her.

"Not yours!"

"Who else knows you are here?"

"Why does it have to be anyone's business but my own?"

"You know why. Because you are taking a ridiculous and unnecessary risk."

"Why shouldn't I?" she flared suddenly.

"There are several good reasons," he replied calmly. "Some you know, and some you don't. The ones you know should be enough to convince you. Why don't they?"

It wasn't that the arguments weren't convincing. It was that she couldn't explain to anyone the need she had, to be Hani sometimes.

She had yearned so long to be Shakira that she could hardly herself understand why the transition was sometimes so difficult. She had been Hani for so much of her life, and that part of herself and her life, it seemed, would not simply be banished in the way she wished and her family expected. Hani, she was learning, was a part of who Shakira was. There were things about being Hani that she had enjoyed. Pitting her wits against the world to wrest what she needed from it had given life an edge quite different from what she now experienced in the palace, where anything she wanted was given to her almost before she knew she wanted it.

She could not have put this into words. But she could not resist it, either.

Someone brushed by with a muttered complaint. They were causing a problem with traffic flow, standing here, and he took her arm and led her towards the entrance and the beautiful golden dome.

He smiled, trying to disconnect her hostility.

"Where did you get that costume?"

She shrugged. "I traded for it with one of the boys here. How did you know I was here?"

"Last Thursday I saw you by chance. Today I followed you from the palace. And yesterday. You are taking too much risk, Shakira, and it has to stop. If your own safety doesn't warrant it, think of your family."

"Leave me alone! Mind your own business, Sharif! If I'm doing something wrong, I've got family to advise me!"

He almost laughed. "You've just admitted that they don't know what you're doing. Shall I tell Ash about it, so he can advise you?"

"Are you threatening me?"

"You can't have it both ways!" he snapped, suddenly losing his grip. "You don't want me giving you advice, but unless I tell someone, who else is there?"

"I know what I'm doing! I don't need advice."

"No, you don't, and yes, you do."

She glared at him, torn between rage at being treated as if she had a secret vice, and embarrassment at having one.

"Leave me alone, goat molester!" she cried in what he recognized as the camp *patois,* and he realized suddenly that she reverted to it whenever she felt cornered.

"No, nor camels, either," he said, his eyes glinting in a way that secretly made her flinch. All the more reason to stand up to the threat.

"Who would ever guess you were so civilized?" she said rudely.

"And to think I once thought you had a way with insult. Can't you do better than that?"

"With an interesting subject, I might!"

He smiled a slow, dangerous smile, and Shakira tensed for action. "If you were really the boy you're pretending to be, I would teach you something about the dangers of insulting those who are bigger than you are. Be careful—if you're too good in your role I might forget."

She snorted. "Do you think I don't know what it's like to be kicked around by bullies? Go ahead and try, but I warn you, I haven't forgotten *everything* I learned in the camps."

"You haven't forgotten any of it, by what I see!" Sharif snapped, annoyed to find that he had lost his temper. "What are you doing here, you little fool? Yearning for the hell you couldn't wait to leave? Wishing I had left you there?"

It was just what her own guilt was constantly telling her, and to hear it from another—from Sharif Azad al Dauleh, of all people—was more than she could bear.

"Maybe you should have!" she cried. "Maybe I'm not good enough! What am I? I'm nothing! I'm not worth bothering about! And who asked you? Not me!"

Then, with a sudden sob, she was at the heart of the matter.

"First they made me forget Shakira to become Hani, and now I have to forget Hani to become Shakira! Always I have to forget who I am! But I am a human being! I am everything that I am! My life and my history—I can't pretend I have not been who I was! Who I still am!"

He glanced around. Her raised voice was drawing the interested glances of two men struggling with a cart full of gold-embroidered velvet, and a woman who had stopped to ask them where their stall was.

"I understand," he said softly. "But sometimes things that are not pleasant must be said, and listened to. You are not in the camp now, isolated and alone. What you do has impact on more than yourself, Shakira, and there could—"

"Leave me alone!" Shakira cried, and turned and fled back into the bazaar.

As though the incident had been some kind of trigger, Shakira was suddenly Angry. With a capital *A*. Her anger bubbled up ten times a day, without warning, without reason, leaving her shaken and disturbed, and everyone else cowering. Any innocent comment might set it off. Any slightest suggestion seemed to be an attempt to curb her, to make her into someone she was not, to make her conform.

She reacted accordingly. The anger tore through her like a whirlwind. She couldn't control her rages any more than she could have told the storm to still.

Sometimes, when she was in a rage, she blamed Sharif for all this. It was because he had tried to make her deny Hani, as she had once been forced to deny Shakira. He had followed her, threatened her. He had put her in the wrong for being herself, just the way her stepmother had. He thought because he had rescued her that he owned her. He thought he could tell her what to do.

And it didn't help that she now couldn't seem to escape his presence. Given the size of the ancient palace, it was nothing short of miraculous the way she kept running into Sharif. He was just around the corner when she turned it, or just down the corridor when she entered it, or crossing the courtyard as she looked down. It was as if fate itself was determined that they should meet.

He was never afraid of her rages. Whether she was raging at someone else, or at him, he simply looked at her, so that she suddenly became aware of what she was doing. Sometimes it enraged her even further. Sometimes she was abashed.

"I told you to stop following me around!" she cried, finding him in the courtyard when she came down one morning.

Sharif frowned. "Princess, even members of the royal family—your cousin might say *especially* members of the royal family—have a duty to speak to other people with respect."

"I call it a lack of respect for you to follow me. So if you didn't, you wouldn't get treated with a lack of respect!"

He stood looking at her with that grave expression, and her anger damped a little, and she was ashamed. He was a Cup

Companion, a noble man on his own merits, and he had found her and saved her from a life of torment.

Then she recovered. "It makes me angry when every time I look up, you're there."

"But then, everything makes you angry at the moment, doesn't it, Princess?"

She wished she could jump on him, and bite and punch him, the way she had the guards at the camp when they harassed her. She gazed at him, confused, bewildered, in turmoil.

"Princess, you are still going to the bazaar as Hani," he said.

She put up a shoulder. "So what if I am?"

"Your cousin has enemies, Shakira. Be careful that you do not offer them ammunition. Is that how you wish to repay his kindness and care?"

Eleven

Something that became a handy focus for her rage was the question of the Gulf Islands. Farida was still living in the palace, and growing more unhappy with every passing week. There was no news of her husband.

But though the Princess raged and stormed, there was going to be no quick solution. It was a complex problem, as she found out when an exasperated Sultan thrust a thick dossier at her.

"Read that, Cousin," he ordered. "And then, and only then, will I listen to further argument on the subject!"

Shakira already knew much of what she read at first. About a decade before, Ghasib had leased an island to a company called Mystery Resorts, who subsequently built an expensive hotel—the Gulf Eden Resort—on it. This had been a successful venture, so successful that the company had wanted to expand to the other islands in the chain, planning to offer exclusive isolated holidays on the beautiful islands.

For that, they needed the islands empty. And two years ago, Ghasib had leased all the other islands in the chain to the company, with the contractual right to evacuate the inhabitants. His government had even helped in the evacuation—as Shakira already knew. Farida had told her there were Bagestani soldiers with the Mystery security men when Solomon's Foot had been ruthlessly evacuated.

All the homes had been destroyed.

That had been about eighteen months ago, the time when Farida had come to the camp where she and Hani met. Later they had been moved to Burry Hill together.

So much she knew. The dossier went further. When the Sultan was restored to the throne, Shakira now learned, he immediately revoked the lease which Ghasib had granted for the islands, except for the land that housed the original Gulf Eden Resort. He had announced that the islanders would be brought home, and promised them help rebuilding their homes.

But as the first few families had returned, Mystery Resorts had challenged Ash's revocation of their lease. They argued that the contract had been signed by Ghasib effectively on behalf of the Bagestan nation, and the nation was required to fulfill it. The company had already applied for an injunction to prevent any resettlement by the islanders, and was now threatening the Sultan with a lawsuit.

"Though it's been carefully kept from public knowledge, Mystery Resorts is owned by the powerful multinational which also owns, among many others, the pharmaceutical giant Webson Attary," she read in one briefing. "They may attempt to influence the decision of some of Bagestan's trading partners in the coming trade negotiations. This could have serious implications for the economy."

On another front, the bid to convince the tribal council of mountain and desert tribes to allow the islanders to resettle on the mainland, temporarily or permanently, was running into fierce opposition.

And a new player had entered the game. A conservation group was now declaring that the habitat of the Aswad turtle, a turtle unique to the Gulf Islands and on the endangered species list, was under serious threat. A research paper had criticized the islanders for their trade in turtle shells and other products and warned that the turtle was heading for extinction if the islanders were allowed to return. This group was agitating loudly in the Western media.

"If you have a solution, Shakira, I'll be glad to hear it," the Sultan said, not unkindly, when she put the dossier back on his desk.

"I don't think you have anything to worry about. It's a good sign, isn't it? It's healthy," Dana said.

Shakira stared. "Why do you say that? A good sign?"

"It means you're starting to feel more secure with us. Up till now you haven't felt able to express your feelings about what happened to you, and you must have an awful lot stored up inside. You could hardly go through what you've gone through without feeling pretty furious at the world. And I think it has to come out. Now that you feel safer, you can let it out."

"I don't see that!" Shakira cried, annoyed by this assessment.

"And the more you trust us, the more it will feel safe to let it out." Dana smiled. "You spent years of your childhood in mostly inhuman conditions, Shakira, at a time when other children were being loved and cherished. Of course you were angry at being treated like that. You're human, you had a right to be treated with respect and dignity, and something in you knew it. And now you are telling the world about it."

"I did express it then!" Shakira cried, as if she had been accused of cowardice. "I was angry lots of times! People were afraid of me, you know!" She sounded as if it were something to be proud of, and in the camps it had been.

"I can see why," the Sultana admitted. "You're pretty fierce when you're fierce. Well, then, perhaps it needs to be expressed again. You're also used to defending yourself against all comers. You were alone and defenceless and if you hadn't learned that behaviour you wouldn't have survived. It's very stressful trying to learn new patterns of behaviour, I'm sure of that. And you won't do that overnight."

"And I was not defenceless! I could look after myself very well."

Dana just kept smiling, with that warm approving glow in her dark eyes that Shakira found totally unnerving when she was in this mood.

"Go easy on yourself, Shakira. You can't change completely overnight, you know. Inside—" she reached over and put a finger against the princess's heart "—inside there's still a lot of Hani, you know. You can't just toss him away. He needs to feel loved, too."

Shakira snorted. "Nobody loves Hani."

Dana laughed outright, but it was a gentle laugh. "Oh, yes. We all love Hani. We see him quite a lot, you know. Maybe more than you think. Ask anyone."

"Love him?" she whispered.

"Everybody loves him. He's funny, and sharp, and he doesn't take anything from anybody. And he's good— painfully good—at pointing it out when the emperor isn't wearing any clothes."

Shakira looked around, as if to make sure she was still in the same room. She swallowed, then straightened her shoulders. "Sharif doesn't love Hani!" she burst out.

"Oh, I think he does. In fact, just the other day he said—"

"What? What did he say?"

"Now, what was it—you were asking Bari and Noor about Solomon's Foot, weren't you? Farida's island, where they were castaway. And he said, 'When she learns to harness all that energy she'll be formidable.' And he was smiling as if you'd been worth every second of the trouble he took to find you."

Shakira was shaking, her anger lost in confusion. "I don't understand," she whispered.

Dana looked into her eyes. "Shakira, Hani is the person who kept you alive all those years, till we found you. Of course we love him—and whatever he had to do and be to fight the good fight, we respect that. And thank him. And if he wants to rage around and tell the world what he thinks of the way you were treated all those years—well, he's got that right, don't you think?"

Was it as simple as that? Shakira wondered later, walking in the beautiful courtyard where her soul, however disturbed, always found some peace. After two weeks of storms, the anger died. The day after her conversation with the Sultana, she woke up knowing it had passed.

She still had a temper, of course, she was still her volatile self, but the overwhelming rages were gone, as suddenly as they had come.

Shakira stood on her balcony watching the dawn. It was a beautiful time for the garden, when the pool was completely smooth and still, perfectly reflecting the cascading squinches of the dome.

Across the garden, Sharif's light told her that he was awake. Just like those first days after her arrival at the palace, when she had stood here waiting for him to appear.

As she watched, the sun climbed up behind the dome to kiss the treetops with gold. The *bulbul* sang to the still-unawakened rose, and suddenly her own heart clenched with yearning—but for what she hardly knew.

As if in answer to her question, Sharif appeared on his balcony, lighting a thin black cigar. He stood for a moment gazing across at her and, in the moment before he lifted his hand in greeting, some knowledge trembled on the border of consciousness—a terrible knowledge it must have been, for her heart was suddenly beating hard.

Feeling surged up in her, and she knew suddenly that Sharif

could explain the confusion she felt when she thought of him. If she was ever brave enough to ask.

There was something else she could ask him, though, and her questions were long overdue.

"What is it you want to know?" Sharif asked.

"You said—you said, 'Your cousin has enemies. Be careful you don't offer them ammunition.'"

He blew a cloud of smoke and looked down at her.

"Tell me," Shakira said urgently.

The sun gleamed from her dark, thick lashes, and worry shaded her eyes, and he realized suddenly that there was nothing she could ask that he would not give her. And that he should have known it long ago.

But that was not the question she had asked.

"How much do you know about the Gulf Islands, Princess?" he began softly.

She stared. "The Gulf Islands! What have the…" She took a deep breath and calmed down. "I read a dossier Ash gave me."

He nodded. "Then I suppose you got most of it. Did you learn about the environmental group?"

She snorted, because it was scarcely believable. "Turtles! It's ridiculous that people should be made homeless because of that, isn't it?" she cried. "What do *they* know about being driven from your home in the middle of the night and then not being allowed to go back?"

He was silent, and she looked up to find him gazing down at her, with a smile lurking behind his eyes.

"Nothing," he said softly.

Her heart kicked a little, and she looked away to where the sunrise was turning the sky pink behind the shadowed dome.

"The campaign is nevertheless serving to whip up a certain amount of world opinion against the resettlement of the island tribes," Sharif went on, calmly. "And world opinion is something we can't afford to lose on this issue. Especially now."

She was quick to pick up on his tone.

"What's happened?"

"We have inside information that Mystery Resorts is about to launch their lawsuit. They intend to sue the Sultan and people of Bagestan for twenty-five billion dollars."

"Camel stuffers!" she cried, outraged, and then, incredulously, "Twenty-five *billion?*"

He ground out his cigar in the earth under a potted plant. "That's bigger than the entire gross national product of Bagestan."

"But I don't understand it—they can't build the resort now, can they? That would damage the ecosystem as much as…it doesn't make sense!"

Approval of her quickness glinted in the Cup Companion's eyes.

"You would think so. But it may be that they feel they can buy off the environmentalists by promising habitat protection for the turtles, or by big funding for some environmental issue elsewhere. So we imagine. Or it's possible the group was deliberately funded to mount the turtle campaign by the company itself, in order to bring more pressure to bear on Ash."

A silence fell, punctuated by the *bulbul's* singing, while Shakira absorbed it. Ash seemed to be trapped as surely as if he were surrounded by barbed wire fences in the middle of a desert.

"There must be *something* we can do!" she cried desperately.

"It is crucially important to prevent them from launching the suit, because once that's in motion, the whole issue will be tied up in the courts for years. We are going to mount a public relations campaign, Princess, in the hopes that public opinion will make Mystery Resorts think twice about the lawsuit."

Shakira watched as the sun's fingers at last reached the water of the pool, stroking the still surface without raising a ripple.

"And is that everything?" she asked thoughtfully.

He was silent, and she looked up.

"What connection does this have with Hani, Sharif? Ammunition, you said. Give Ash's enemies ammunition."

"Not exactly ammunition. But the palace has worked very hard to keep the media away from you till you are stronger, with the result that everyone is frothing at the mouth for a story. I'm sure you've seen the paparazzi hanging around the palace gates. After all our work on the campaign it would be a tragedy, wouldn't it, if the story gripping the world's media about Bagestan wasn't the plight of the Gulf Island exiles, but how Princess Shakira secretly dresses as her former self and hangs around the bazaar begging for sweets and causing mischief."

3
Princess

The Princess's Dream

In the dream she strapped on a sword, mounted a white horse, took a banner in her hand, and rode into battle to free her people from oppression. There were bright lights on the battlefield, blazing down on her, blinding her so that she could hardly see the enemy.

People came to watch the battle. They sat by the battlefield, in rows and rows, hundreds and thousands of strangers. They cheered and applauded when they saw her arrive. They called her name, and urged her on.

The battle was strange and confusing, in the dream, for many times she could not see the enemy at all, but only shouted and called to him in a swirling fog, as her horse plunged nervously, and her people cried out for deliverance. Tiny red eyes followed her everywhere in the gloom, as if the Invisible itself watched her struggle.

Then, suddenly, a messenger brought her a letter. It was a message announcing victory.

All around her, the battlefield broke out in cheering.

Twelve

BOY PRINCESS TO DEBUT AT
PALACE RECEPTION

Tomorrow the royal family will host a reception for Bagestan's "lost" princess, to introduce her to the extended royal family and foreign notables.

The reception is a prelude to her entering on public life. Princess Shakira will embark on a limited number of public duties and appearances, the palace announced, mainly for the Gulf Island Refugee Support Group.

The Princess, who, to escape Ghasib's assassins, spent her life in refugee camps disguised as a boy until her discovery several months ago, is now a patron of the charity. The plight of the islanders, who are prevented from returning to their homes by the presence on the Gulf Islands of an endangered turtle species, is said to touch her very closely.

"**O**h, Shakira! Aren't you staggering! Kamila, you've outdone yourself this time!" Noor cried.

The designer smiled and tweaked a fold.

Shakira was too stunned to speak. She just kept staring and staring at the vision in the mirror.

The ruby-red harem pants were of diaphanous silk, laced with intricate embroidery, and studded with pearls and rubies. Waist and ankles were both belted with a wide, primitive band of thickly clustered gemstones in shades of red entwined with gold thread; a matching bracelet snugly encircled one slender, graceful wrist.

Above, a silk spaghetti-strap bodice left her arms and shoulders bare. From its waist a long skirt fell in layers of gauzy ruby-coloured silk open at the front from the hem to just above her navel. A neat triangle of bare flesh was revealed between the jewelled belt of the harem trousers and the bodice. Even standing still, the silky skirt seemed to billow around her. On her feet, the delicate ruby-and-diamanté straps crossing each instep were more jewellery than sandal.

A swarm of helpers buzzed around her, tweaking and adjusting, but Shakira scarcely noticed their ministrations.

She was glowing with the aftermath of a day of manicure, pedicure, massage and facial. The makeup artist had done wonderful things for her already large eyes, making them smoky and mysterious; her full mouth was glossed with only a hint of colour; her nails were French polished, her toenails ruby-red. Her hair was a mass of glossy curls swept back from her forehead and down the back of her neck to reveal the high, proud al Jawadi cheekbones and well-shaped ears. Ruby-and-diamond ear studs in a primitive cluster caught a mountain of light every time she breathed.

A single curl fell over her forehead.

"You look like a—oh, I don't know who you look like!" Noor exclaimed, as words failed her. "Like yourself, I think.

Like the woman you were always meant to be. You're going to knock him flat!"

"Who?"

In the mirror, Jalia and Noor exchanged a slightly alarmed glance.

"Everybody!"

"Who has come?" Shakira asked nervously. "Are the—my family here?"

The two cousins laughed delightedly. "Darling, of course they are! Who would miss this? I heard that people were practically killing for an invitation, but of course everyone with the least excuse to be called family got one, and if you think anyone would—they're all here, Shakira," Noor assured her earnestly. "Of course they are."

One was missing, but Shakira kept that thought to herself. It was not fair to her family to continually regret her brother's absence.

"Prince Omar and Crown Prince Kavian and their wives you know about already." Jalia was listing on her fingers. "A handful of international celebrities who were active in Bagestani Drought Relief. Every single one accepted. The media are out in force. The paparazzi are thick as thieves around the main gate."

Noor looked at her watch. "It's time."

Guards in fabulous dress uniform saluted as she passed through the massive arched doorway onto the huge domed *talar* that overlooked the entire length of the Great Court.

Shakira had previously seen the Great Court only in daylight. Now she stood gazing out over the vista in stunned wonder. Never in her life, never in her richest dreams, had she conjured up a vision of such magnificence.

In the centre of the courtyard, four square pools, each with a fountain playing in the centre, were surrounded with flaming torches that caused the tumbling water to shimmer like an endless stream of diamonds. On three sides, the columns of cloisters and balconies were also lighted by paired torches. Stepped water channels looked like ribbons of silver and gold threading between the lush trees and thickly flowered shrubs.

The ceiling and columns of the *talar*, studded with mirrored mosaic embedded in old gold and glimmering with torchlight, gave the place the enchantment of a fairy castle. At the far end of the courtyard the dome was dark and shadowy. Beyond it, the golden dome of the mosque shimmered. Above, moon and stars in the lush, purple-black sky contributed their lustre and magic.

The courtyard was jammed with a crowd of people dressed in rich colours, lavishly embroidered with gold, whose jewels glowed and sparkled, indiscriminately reflecting torchlight and starlight, as the crowd flowed in channels like the water.

Shakira entered in the wake of the Sultan and Sultana, and awareness seemed to whisper through the crowd, so that, one by one, and then in clusters and whole groups, they turned to stare as she gazed, all unconsciously, at the dreamscape.

A collective gasp of delighted approval breathed through them. So this was the boy princess, the lost child!

She was completely unexpected: the most beautiful of urchins. A particularly beguiling page stepped straight from the *Nights,* staring at them like Aladdin's first visit to the cave of treasure.

When she came to herself again, the Sultan and Sultana had gone down into the court, and she was alone on the platform, and the object of everyone's focused attention. Shakira blinked. Then her wide, startled smile enchanted even further, and the air suddenly resounded with a sudden, spontaneous outburst of applause and cheering.

"Brava, Princess!"

She breathed to steady herself as her eyes searched the uplifted faces for those she knew and loved.

The Sultan was tall and handsome in a red silk jacket with ropes of pearls over his chest and a long swath of gold cloth over one shoulder, a proud smile softening his stern face. Beside him Dana, her hair piled in an intricate chignon braided with a diamond-and-gold rope, wearing an elegantly simple white *shalwar kamees,* gold sandals and a gold scarf, was also smiling warmly at her.

Her grandmother Suhaila, in emerald-green and gold, stood proud and confident beside that tall imposing couple, like the star she was. Her eyes were black jewels flashing approval.

The rest of the family were mingled with the crowd. Shakira's eyes roved the faces. Noor and Jalia beside their handsome, dark-eyed fiancés, Noor's brothers, the Sultan's sisters, and all the others she had met over the past months—cousins, aunts, uncles, and more remote connections. All family. For so many years she had been alone. Now her family numbered in the dozens, and in their faces she saw that they were proud of her, and her heart swelled and was filled with sweetness as she gazed at them, and felt a part of that larger whole. Felt how she belonged.

She started down the steps then, the silk skirt of her costume rippling around her as a sudden soft breeze whispered up the steps just for this moment, for her. Her eyes kept moving, searching for one more face.

He was standing by himself beside a shooting fountain, handsome in a midnight-dark silk jacket draped with pearls and gold, his black hair glinting in the light that painted a thousand curls.

Sharif was not smiling. His eyes were a reflection of the night sky, his jaw was tight, and he was staring at her as if he knew he'd been shot and was waiting to feel the pain.

All unconsciously, the Princess smiled and reached out a hand towards him, and he was powerless to resist the unspoken, unconscious request. Ignoring court protocol, the Cup Companion stepped forward to help the Princess down the steps to the courtyard.

Around them the whispers started.

He's the man who rescued her. Without him she wouldn't be here.

Is it going to be a match?
Just look at her face!
Look at his.

She stood looking up at him in the semidarkness, deaf to everything, while torchlight flickered around her, an elfin creature. He might have been dreaming. He had looked at the photo of the child and dedicated himself to finding her and knowing what kind of woman she had become. He had not understood then that he had fallen in love with the woman she would be. That was why he had had to find her.

He smiled, though he didn't feel like smiling. He wanted to wrap her in his arms and swear to cherish and protect her forever. The thought made him realize that he was still holding her hand, but he could not let it go.

Her own mouth curved, her eyes reflecting the flickering torchlight, as if he had rubbed a magic lamp and wished.

"Well?" she said, offering herself with that touching lack of feminine guile that marked all she did.

Her big, dark eyes still dominated her face, and the intensity of her character was imprinted there, and he saw that it would never fade. Shakira would always care deeply.

The full mouth was made for passion, but it was too soon to tell her so, too soon to teach her mouth the ways of love. Her flesh, firm with health, glowed in the warm light, the skin of her thighs shimmering as tantalizingly through the sheer silk of the harem pants as did the pearls and rubies of the embroidery.

He clenched his jaw for a moment, struggling to keep the intensity of feeling from his eyes.

"Very well, Princess," he approved softly, and torchlight also glinted in his eyes. "Very, very well. But aren't you meant to be meeting Prince Omar?"

"Yes, in a moment. But I wanted to show you first. They will understand," she said, blithely dismissing protocol with the flick of a hand. "It's a big change from the boy you nearly ran down on the road, isn't it?"

"But although Shakira is a very beautiful woman, I think I still see traces of Hani deep in her eyes."

She caught her breath. "Beautiful?"

His eyes went dark, and he struggled with himself. "Don't you have a mirror?" he asked roughly. The impact of her suddenly-revealed femininity, combined with her own complete unconsciousness of its power, dragged at his self-control.

"That isn't the same as hearing you say it," she confided.

Behind her he saw, almost with relief, the smiling Sultana bearing down on them, and he lifted the still-slender hand and bent to drop a kiss on it as they parted.

The kiss burned her skin for long after she left him. As if she had been shocked with a jolt of electricity, and the nerves of her arm—her whole body—were constantly remembering it.

The Sultana had decreed an informal reception, so that rather than being in a receiving line, Shakira was introduced to people easily as she and her grandmother, Ash and Dana moved through the crowd. Several times as she was led from group to group and introduced, she looked back, trying to find Sharif, to try to read from his face what he had meant by the kiss, but he was lost in the crowd.

She was introduced to Crown Prince Kavian of Parvan, Shahbanu Alinor, and their eldest son, Prince Roshan, along with Prince Omar of Central Barakat and his wife, Princess Jana. In the days when all the al Jawadis had lived in disguise, Ashraf had been Omar's most trusted Cup Companion. He had even followed him into battle when the Prince had taken a company of Cup Companions to fight on Kavian's side after the Kaljuk invasion of Parvan led to the terrible war.

Shakira knew all about that.

"Your country gave us asylum," she told Kavian. "My stepmother was always so grateful. She was very frightened when we had nowhere to go except Bagestan. But at the last minute Parvan accepted us."

"I am sorry we could not take better care of you," said Kavian. They all saw her face change, remembering, and the subject was quickly changed.

Of course everyone at the party, family or not, wanted to meet the lost princess, and after an hour or two, Shakira began visibly to wilt.

"It must be hard for you to be in such a large crowd," someone offered sympathetically.

"It is a much more pleasant crowd than the goat molesters you find around a water delivery truck, trampling the women and children who are waiting for something to drink," Shakira said trenchantly. She still did not like any suggestion implying weakness on her part.

"Oh! Ah…yes, I imagine so!"

With a smile Dana turned to Suhaila and said softly, "I think we might start now."

The singer lifted her hands in agreement, and a few minutes later ascended to the *talar*. The band of *tar* and *zitar*, *nay* and *santur*, the traditional instruments of Suha's backing group, played a stirring introduction of the familiar notes, and in her clear, haunting voice, Suha sang the first electrifying notes of *Aina al Warda*.

Where is the Rose?
When will I see her?
The nightingale asks after his Beloved….

He came and found her then, for she was the Rose to him and he could not resist. They walked in the gardens, saying little.

A gust of wind caught the spray of a fountain and blew it over them, bringing with it the scent of roses, and Shakira stopped and lifted her face to the spray.

"Oh!" she cried, and was still for a long moment, her eyes shut. Then she turned to him, saying softly, "Do you remember I told you about my parents' garden, and the spray of water in my face?"

"I remember," Sharif said, his voice deep with feeling because her mouth trembled between grief and joy.

"It must have been just like this, don't you think? A gust of wind blowing…that's why I remember both the drops of water and the scent of roses…."

"Yes." His heart was full of a thousand things, but he could not voice them now.

"Sometimes, in the camps, I thought that—that I'd never again be as happy as I remembered being then. But it wasn't true, Sharif," she whispered, her eyes glistening with moonlight as she smiled at him in delighted, wondering discovery, as if he were an essential ingredient of her happiness. "It wasn't true."

Thirteen

"**M**y best advice would be to start with one or two local interviews, so the Princess can get her bearings," Gazi al Hamzeh said. "Then we'll go straight for a top international chat show and ditto for a print interview. How do you feel about that, Princess?"

Gazi was an old friend of the Sultan's, an expert PR man, Cup Companion to Prince Karim of West Barakat. He had masterminded the media campaign during Ashraf's successful bid to unseat Ghasib, and now he was being drafted in to manage Shakira's public launch as spokeswoman for the Gulf Island Refugees.

Shakira rubbed her nose. Sometimes she seemed to be in the middle of a dream. "All right. Do you think anyone will want me?"

Gazi sat for a moment looking as if he didn't really believe her. Then he grinned. "The world wants you, Princess. We'll send you out as a double act with Sharif—the man who rescued a princess from a refugee camp. This one's so hot it's smoking."

* * *

There was one thing that she hadn't yet done, and one morning Shakira set out from the palace, accompanied by Sharif, to return to her childhood home.

It was in a pretty village some miles from the capital, in the foothills of the mountains. "It was the summer residence of some nobleman," her grandmother had told her, in one of their many conversations about family history. "Safa bought it and gave it to me when Mahlouf was born. He did not want Mahlouf's future to be dependent on Majdi's generosity. Majdi did not like the idea much, but we spent our summers there before the coup.

"Mahlouf was determined to return to Bagestan when he grew up, to live in the home that his father had given him. Probably the house was all the clue Ghasib's spies needed to discover who Mahlouf really was. And they bided their time."

"Be prepared for it not to be as you remembered it," Sharif advised her now, as the car passed through the little village. He had visited the village during his search for her brother. "The house will have suffered, too."

Perhaps that was why she had waited before coming here. Sometimes she had thought that she could never bear to come and see the remains of the dream that had sustained her through so much. But unless her brother appeared, which seemed less and less likely as time passed, the house belonged to her now. And she would have to decide what to do about it.

They turned into a side street that ran uphill for a short stretch and then stopped. On the right, by a long, high, once-white wall, they stopped. Shakira got out and stood in front of a weather-beaten door. So far nothing seemed in the least familiar.

"Are you sure this is it?" she asked foolishly.

He understood. "It's not surprising if you don't recognize the exterior, Shakira. You were only six when you left."

The door was locked, but Sharif had come prepared. He produced a crowbar from the car. "When I was here, the villagers told me one of Ghasib's generals had been living here until he ran foul of his boss and was imprisoned or executed. The family fled, and the house has been empty for years. No one dared to come in."

He put a finger on the bell. "But we will make sure."

He kept his finger on the bell for several seconds. They couldn't hear the bell ringing, and there was no sound of footsteps, so after a couple of minutes Sharif began to tap the crowbar into the jamb against the lock. It gave, and a moment later the door swung open onto a shadowed vestibule.

Shakira slowly lifted a foot and stepped inside.

She wasn't sure what made her look up; to find the source of the shadowy light, perhaps. High overhead was a stained glass dome with a delicate blue pattern that was just visible against the dead leaves and other debris that clogged it.

"Oh, it is the right place!" she whispered, for she had stood and craned her neck to see that beauty overhead before. It was closer now, because she was taller, and some of the pieces of the mosaic were broken and missing, but she knew it.

Ahead was another door, this time unlocked. She opened it and peered down the gloomy corridor behind. Sharif following behind her, the Princess began to trace the corridor. Sloping down from street level, it zigged and zagged.

"It's typical of houses of the period. It's so that the women and children cannot be seen from the street," Sharif said when she wondered at it.

After about fifty feet the corridor opened onto desolation. The pool and garden of her memory were there in outline and shape, she saw at once, but the fierce wind of neglect, and worse, had blasted them. The courtyard was a spread of ruin. Stagnant water, fallen brick, cracked paving, faded tiles and, over all, a thick layer of dead leaves, twigs, rubble and torn paper, through which were sticking up the skeletons of the trees that had once shaded and blessed the space.

Enclosing the courtyard on two sides were delicate arched

windows and doors, several broken, with the intricate stained glass frame inserts showing the effects of neglect and the battering of the elements. The walls that surrounded and surmounted them were covered by panels of stone and plaster that had once been decorated with a breathtaking richness of design. Now it was faded, chipped, and broken.

But still the ghost of what had been was strong.

She stood for several minutes staring at it, measuring it against the garden of her memory. "Something so beautiful. Why did they let this happen?" she whispered, but Sharif only shook his head. He had no more answer than she.

He held out his hand, and she gratefully took it. "It's not as bad as it looks," he said, casting an eye at the roofing and the walls. "Structurally the place looks sound, and most of what is needed is cosmetic. With the right artisans, it could be fully restored."

"I'm glad you're with me," she said softly. His eyes darkened, and he looked as though he was about to speak, but changed his mind.

They went into the house then, and walked through room after room where once artists had painted dazzling scenes on the walls. Scenes of lovers' meetings, of the chase, of the forest, scenes from the lives of heroes and kings taken from the great national myth of Bagestan.

All were in more or less disrepair. Windows and doors had been left open to the elements at some time, and some of the furniture was damaged and waterlogged.

And yet, the house was beautiful. Even the trace of what it had been was enough to make the breath catch in her throat. Domed ceilings cascaded down in an ever increasing spread of squinches like a frozen chord of music, painted with perfect delicacy. As in parts of the palace, glass doors framed with mosaics of stained glass slid upwards to create an opening onto the courtyard, so that a wall the entire length of a room could disappear upwards and leave the room open-sided.

"It is a beautiful house," Sharif murmured as they stood in one such opening and gazed out at the courtyard. "No wonder you never forgot this."

"Look!" she cried suddenly, for on one of the trees at the far end of the courtyard, nearest the once-beautiful *talar* and its exquisite domed ceiling, something pink clung to the end of a blasted branch. Shakira began to pick her way through the debris, walking by the edge of the clogged reflecting pool where once, the pattern of the tiles visible under the choke of leaves told her, a path had been.

"That's me," she whispered when they had reached the tree. A rosebud, against all the odds, was alive, on one green twig. "That's me, the last flower of a tree that…that…" She shut her eyes tight, for the memory of those last days with her brother was very strong here.

"Oh, where is my brother? Why can't we find him? Did I dream it?"

But again Sharif was helpless and had no answer for her.

She remembered something suddenly, and went back inside, moving through the rooms until she came to a door she knew. Her heart leapt in her throat as she opened it, and she stood on the threshold, staring in.

Her father's massive wooden desk was still there, where it had always been, looking different only because she was taller now. *Bismillah arrahman arraheem.* She heard the murmur of his voice in the rustle of leaves in the wind that gusted through the broken window.

"Man antom?" growled a voice in the guttural country dialect. *Who are you?*

Shakira gasped and whirled. Behind her, in the doorway, Sharif was looking down at an old man. The man was stocky but thin-faced, with thick, stiff grey hair, dark eyes and a wide mouth.

"The owner of the house has come to inspect it," Sharif said firmly. "Who are you?"

"The owner? What owner? Everyone is dead," said the old man.

Shakira gasped as the voice and face together stirred some latent memory to life. "Mister Gulab!" she cried, the name seeming to come out of her mouth without any participation from her brain.

He came closer and peered into the room past Sharif.

"Who is it?"

"I am Shakira, Mister Gulab! Do you remember me? Shakira al Nadim, the daughter of Mahlouf and Saira." It still gave her a thrill to pronounce the names. "You were—you worked in my mother's rose garden, didn't you?"

The old man stared at her under his bushy white eyebrows, his head thrust forward. Then his arms went up in amazement.

"*Ya Allah!* Shakira! Khanum Shakira!" the old man cried. "You are alive? *Alhamdolillah!* God be praised, for He willed it so! So long it has been! And now you are a woman! And what of your brother?" He turned to Sharif. "Is this Mazin, who also, God be thanked, escaped the murderous villains who killed your family?"

"The other servants fled," Gulab explained a little later, as he served them mint tea in tiny gold-rimmed glasses set in gold holders. "Here is the sugar. Drink it sweet, Khanum Shakira, for your heart has suffered much today, seeing the house the way it never was in the days of the old Sultan, peace be upon him. Do you recognize these glasses? They were your mother's favourite set. I borrowed them many years ago, may she forgive me."

"They fled?" Shakira prompted, obediently dropping two cubes into her cup. She looked around at the gardener's room, and remembered that this was not the first time she had drunk mint tea here. Strange how the memories that had so defiantly refused to arise in her before were now coming back, as if they existed in the air itself and her mind merely picked them up.

Gulab sat down on a cushion and picked up his own tea.

"They were frightened, and besides, there was no one to pay their wages. They fled that same night, though I argued that you and Mazin needed someone to cook and look after you."

"He *was* there, then!" Shakira cried. "Sometimes I thought it was just my imagination."

The dark eyes rested on her. "He was a brave boy, your brother. I told him that there was danger, for who knew when Ghasib's men might come to check for just such a possibility, that some had escaped the assassination?"

"You knew that it wasn't an accident?"

"We knew that your father, Mahlouf, was the grandson of the Sultan," he said simply. "It was a secret, but we knew."

"Gulab," she said, after a little reminiscence, "do you know what happened the night I—I was taken away? Do you know what happened to Mazin?"

The grizzled old head nodded. "I had sent a message to…certain people," he said, still retaining the caution he had learned in the Ghasib years, "telling them the situation. Someone came after dark. It was a dangerous mission and they could not risk being seen by some in the village. Arif Bahrami and his wife came themselves. They meant to take the boy, who would be most at risk from Ghasib. Their younger son had died and they hoped they could put Mazin in his place. But when they saw Mazin, they said it would not work. He was too old. He was the same age as their older son, and someone would notice if they suddenly had another boy that age. They wondered about taking you, and giving you their son's name."

Shakira stared, her heart thumping wildly at the explanation. "Is *that* why I had to be a boy! Oh, why didn't they ever explain?"

"Mazin was very brave. He told them to take you, and he would find a way by himself. Bahrami warned him not to stay in the house—to hide in the mountains or the desert, if necessary, because they had information that the secret police already knew that a child had escaped.

"The next night Mazin took a pack with food and water and

said goodbye to me. That was the last I saw him. He was twelve years old, and very brave. Perhaps he was strong enough to survive. It will be as God willed it."

Tears streamed down Shakira's cheeks as he spoke. Into the mountains alone. Oh, Mazin.

Fourteen

"**W**ill you welcome, please—Princess Shakira Warda Jawad al Nadim, and Sheikh Sharif ibn Bassam Azad al Dauleh!"

The applause was polite but not enthusiastic. A spotlight began playing on the carpet just beyond the entrance to the studio, and she knew it was for her. Her heart was beating much louder than the hundreds of clapping hands. She glanced uncertainly up into Sharif's face. He leaned down and said into her ear, "There's nobody out there Hani can't handle with one arm in a sling!"

She snorted with laughter, hastily stifled it, and stepped out into the spot with her head flung up, eyes sparkling, her mouth curving impishly. Sharif followed close behind. The hungry eyes of the cameras glowered at her from several places on the set, near and far, as the chat show hostess came to meet them.

"Well, Princess," she said when they were all seated and the applause had died down. "In the space of a few months, you've been swept from the lowest depths to the absolute pinnacle. You were in a refugee camp in the middle of the Australian desert, an orphan, hungry, and pretending to be a boy. Now you're a princess in one of the most popular Middle Eastern royal families of modern times. You live in a palace, you wear amazing jewels, you travel in a private jet with bodyguards. If you wanted to, you could forget hunger and deprivation ever existed. But you have chosen not to forget."

The hostess smiled at her, but Shakira was remembering, and did not smile back. "It is not a choice," she corrected gravely. "I couldn't forget. I can never forget. I had no home, no name, and no family, and I thought I would never have such things. Now I have everything, but how can I forget what it was like to have nothing? How could I forget the ones who are still there, and still have nothing?"

She shook her head. "I can't forget," she said again.

"We'll talk about the ones who are still there in a moment. But now, tell us what it was like to live in a refugee camp for so many years. It must be dreadful to live under conditions where there are food shortages and even a lack of basic hygiene."

"The worst is not the lack of water and food, or the filth and squalor," Shakira told her earnestly. "The worst is having no name, no history. The worst is when the people talk to you as if you *are* nothing because you have nothing. When a big evil has been done to you, but instead of helping you they make you a prisoner, and treat you as if you are the one who has done the evil. That is the worst. Because they make you, too, think that you are nothing."

"We have some library film of one of the camps you were in," said the hostess gravely, and the audience sat in silence as the footage flashed on the monitor. "Do you recognize this?"

Shakira swallowed hard as first the bleak landscape of makeshift tents and then the familiar shape of a building appeared. She had seen the film before, of course—Gazi al Hamzeh had made sure there would be no surprises tonight. But still it was hard.

"Yes, this is the first camp I was in, in Parvan. At first it was not so bad, but after the invasion the Kaljuks used to bomb and strafe us. But they never hit the kitchen building—that's it there—till right at the end, just before the camp was closed. We all used to run there when the planes came, so when they finally hit it, they killed a lot of people. They killed my stepmother and my stepbrothers and sisters."

A murmur ran through the audience. The camp film clip ended.

"And after that, you were completely alone? How old were you?"

"I don't know. About twelve." Shakira's shoulders moved as if she shrugged off a troublesome feeling.

"And you moved to different camps, all alone, and that's when you pretended to be a boy."

"Yes. It was dangerous to be alone, and a girl. Everyone knows that you have no one to protect you," Shakira admitted reluctantly.

"And you lived as a boy for…what? Nine years?"

The Princess shrugged. "Maybe. I don't remember for sure. It is better not to count birthdays."

"Princess, you've told us what was the worst about your life in those camps. What else do you remember?"

"The politicians who visit and make promises and tell lies," she answered, and the audience clapped their approval.

The hostess smiled. "And after that?"

"Water," said Shakira. "Not in the last camp, not in Australia, but in the others, we had sometimes terrible shortages of clean water. Then you dream of water, night after night. You dream that they have brought in a herd of elephants blowing water over each other's backs. You dream that someone has dug a well…you dream that the babies are not dying anymore."

She turned to gaze out at the studio audience. "To wear jewels, to live in a palace—these things are very pleasant. But to have fresh water to drink, *that* is the—" On a sudden impulse, Shakira pulled off the clasp bracelet she was wearing, and held it out on her palm. Under the studio lights rubies and diamonds sparkled and glowed, and Camera Two greedily closed on it. "Do you think you would not trade that for a sip of pure water in such a place?"

Once more the studio rang with applause. Sitting in the audience, Gazi al Hamzeh leaned to his wife. "She's a natural."

"The man sitting beside you now," the hostess said, "Sheikh Sharif Azad al Dauleh, is the man who hunted for you through a number of those camps, and finally found you."

A smile transformed the small, frowning face. "Yes, then Sharif came. That was a day!"

"Tell us about that, Princess."

"Nothing could be more wonderful than when he came to me and said, *I know your name, and you have a family, and I am going to take you home.* That is the most wonderful thing that ever happened to me in my life."

She suddenly turned to Sharif with a tearful, tremulous smile, and his eyes blazed so fiercely with his uncontrolled response that the audience drew a collective breath. Shakira's own eyes widened, and she seemed trapped by his gaze.

In the audience Gazi let out a slow breath. "Wow."

"I told you so," Anna murmured with a grin.

"It must have been quite a moment for you, too, Your Excellency," the hostess continued after that pregnant moment in which most of the audience seemed to understand much more than had been said.

The black eyes flicked from Shakira's face to the hostess's. "Yes, it was a moment for me, too," he agreed, and everyone heard the understatement.

"But the Princess was masquerading as a boy at the time. How did you know you had found the Princess?"

"I didn't know, at first. I only knew that she was an al Jawadi. And that I knew because she looks like the family. It is a very distinctive thing."

"It's what they call 'the al Jawadi look,' I understand.
We've got some pictures, haven't we? Princess, I think we've
managed to get a photograph of you from the records of the
detention centre where His Excellency found you…"

Something between a gasp and a moan went up from the
studio audience as the gaunt face of Hani flashed up on the
monitors. A thin and hungry boy, his skull too emphasized,
cheeks and temples hollow, eyes ringed with shadow, black
with hostility. A split screen suddenly showed Shakira in the
studio side by side with the Hani photograph.

The contrast between the two faces provoked applause and
cheering, and this time it was prolonged.

"Is that the way the Princess looked the first time you
saw her?"

"Yes, that was Hani," Sharif replied, with a possessive note
in his voice that seemed to wrap her in security. Shakira unconsciously turned to him again, a yearning in her eyes that
all save herself could see.

"Have we got a picture of the Sultan of Bagestan? There
he is."

Ash's face replaced Shakira's beside Hani. "Forgive me,
Excellency, but I don't see much resemblance between that
boy and the Sultan. It's a good thing it wasn't up to me, because I think the Princess might still be in that camp."

More applause and laughter.

"It comes with certain expressions," Sharif explained. "I
was lucky that a particular look on the Princess's face reminded me very strongly of the Sultan."

"It sounds to me as if this was a life-changing experience
for more than the Princess, Excellency," the hostess pressed.
"Was it?"

He turned to look at Shakira, and she smiled again. Possessive hunger burned in him, and he knew he should control
the feeling that showed in his eyes, but could not. He swallowed and opened his mouth, then closed it again.

Again Shakira was lost in his gaze. On the edge of consciousness lay the knowledge that that look in Sharif's eyes was everything she needed, and she smiled all her heart at him.

A murmuring sigh rose from the tiered seats to fill the silence.

"I think I see," commented the hostess, with a smile that sparked the audience into applause.

"Now you're concerned about a particular group of refugees, aren't you, Your Highness?" she continued. "The people called the Gulf Islanders. Can you give us the background?"

Pulling her gaze back to the hostess, Shakira nodded. "Yes. They have a very tragic story." She carefully outlined the situation. "And now they can't go home until the issue of the turtles is settled. So we are working very hard to establish the facts and judge what is the best thing in this situation as quickly as possible. And we also want to convince Mystery Resorts to drop their lawsuit and forget their plans for the islands. Ghasib did not sign that agreement for the people, but for himself. Why should the people now have to honour it?"

"I suppose it's hard for you to understand that something like a rare turtle should keep displaced people from their traditional lands."

Shakira nodded vigorously. "I know how desperate they feel. Other Bagestani refugees are coming home now. Their villages are being rebuilt, but not the islanders'. Maybe we will have to build another camp for them while this argument is decided. How horrible if they have to become refugees in their own country! And where will they go? You can't just put one tribe in the territory of another and tell them to get along.

"Farida, the woman who was my mother in the last camp, is from the island of Solomon's Foot. Her family and her husband's have lived on that island for hundreds, maybe thousands of years. Her husband was arrested and imprisoned by Ghasib on false charges so that the island could be evacuated for Mystery Resorts, and he is still not found. Their home was burned to the ground by the evacuation teams. Farida wants to go back and rebuild, and wait for her husband there. But she has to continue as a refugee."

"And she's staying in the palace with you while she waits?"

"Even in a palace it is hard to be a refugee," Shakira countered firmly. "What good is a palace if it is not your home?"

More applause.

"You know, the turtles have survived alongside the human inhabitants of the islands for thousands of years, or they would not be there now. The islanders have always been very careful of the environment, because they harvest wild herbs for use in their traditional medicines. It is their biggest source of income. People from all over Bagestan use the island herbs."

"What is your own opinion of how this issue should be resolved, then, Princess?"

"Don't go there, Princess," Gazi begged softly. "Remember, 'The claims have to investigated...'"

But in the heat of the moment Shakira forgot his coaching. She threw up her head. "How are the people suddenly a danger to the environment that they have cherished for so long? *I* think this story about the turtles is all made up because Mystery Resorts still want the islands for their exclusive resort. And I think it is evil if they put their profits before a whole people's right to go home."

"Oh!" said the hostess.

"They are just camel-stuffers," said the Princess.

"I'm sorry I got excited," said Shakira. "But why shouldn't I tell the truth? Why shouldn't it be said?"

They were sitting in the hotel suite, watching the broadcast of the show—Shakira and Sharif, Gazi al Hamzeh and his wife, Anna.

"So long as they don't sue for defamation," Gazi said, with humour.

Not a word had been cut. They watched to the end, including the prolonged, enthusiastic applause which guaranteed that the phones would be ringing with new invitations. Lazily scratching his beard shadow, Gazi picked up the remote and shut off the TV. He tossed it down, slapped his hands down on the seat beside him.

"By tomorrow morning we'll have a list of interview requests as long as your arm," he announced. "You did extremely well. Shakira is a natural, and Sharif, you come across with terrific authority. We've got a winning team," he said. "Now let's go out and celebrate."

It was clear from the small buzz that went around the room at their entrance that some of the patrons in the club had watched the show. This was Shakira's first visit to a Western nightclub, so she was staring, too.

"What do people do in a nightclub?" she asked Anna when they were seated.

"Eat, drink, dance, smoke and talk," Anna said succinctly, taking the menu from the waiter. As the other three consulted over the menu, Shakira looked around. The band started playing and people got up to dance.

Shakira watched the dancers for several minutes. "Do you like to dance, Shakira?" Anna asked with a smile.

Shakira smiled and nodded. "We used to dance in the camps sometimes. People had instruments, or they made them, and we would dance when they played. I liked those times—people seemed always happy and laughing." She paused to watch. "I used to think that we didn't do it right, that out in the world dancing would be different. But it's just the same—people jumping around."

Sharif watched the bright eyes for a moment and set his menu aside. "Would you like to jump around now?"

He led her out to the dance floor and Shakira, who, it soon became clear, had inherited a certain musical instinct from her grandmother, began her own particular dance.

She was wearing a dress in emerald-green silk organza, another of Kamila's special designs. A wide jewelled band encircled her throat, the halter-top exposed her shoulders and back. A snug bodice clung to her small breasts and over her stomach to another jewelled band around her hips. The circular skirt was composed of a dozen layers of gauzy silk, the top layer spangled all over with beads and pearls.

Around her ankles her sandals carried matching bands of clustered jewels. The effect, as with most of the wardrobe Kamila had designed for her, was primitive elegance, an effect that was matched now by her part ballet, part belly, part tribal dancing.

Sharif was wearing a tuxedo. "Going native," Gazi and Sharif had called it, when Shakira had challenged their Western evening gear. "Why do men in the West dress like crows?" she'd asked, but no one had an answer. "I don't like it!"

He looked very dark and handsome in the black suit, but Shakira liked him better in the silk jacket and jewels that comprised the dress uniform of the Cup Companions—what he had been wearing the night of the reception given in her honour, when he had told her she was beautiful.

He watched her dance, graceful and unconsciously sensuous, with a tight jaw. Time, he knew. He had to give her time. And yet—there would be plenty of other men now, men who wouldn't necessarily have the patience, or the sense, to give her time. Men were watching her here with eyes that told their own story. If she succumbed to another man while he, Sharif, waited and watched and was careful...

But he would kill any man who came near her.

The sentiment must have been written large on his face, for a man who'd been watching hungrily, catching his eye, suddenly turned to his companion, put his arm around her and leaned into her ear.

The musicians slipped into something slow, and around them the floor emptied. Half a dozen couples remained, moving into each other's arms to begin the slow sway of public sex.

He had waited too long to hold her.

She put her hand in his because he seemed to expect it, but as he drew her closer, she protested nervously, "I never danced with a man before. I don't know what you do."

Then she caught her breath, because Sharif drew her close and put his arm around her. He seemed very tall suddenly: her head just reached his heart, and almost of its own accord nestled there. One arm was around her waist; with the other he held her hand firmly against his chest.

"It's like walking. Shift your weight back and forth between your feet, and let me give you your direction." His voice rumbled in her ear, like a cat's purr, and she felt it all down her spine.

"Oh," she said, on a note of surprise, but she didn't resist, and he wrapped his arm more securely around her, drawing her firmly into his embrace.

She felt enclosed and safe, and a drowsy happiness seemed to flow through her, making her lazy. She did what he had instructed, lifting one foot and then the other, and the movement of his body told hers where to put it down.

The music seemed to flow through them, wrap around them, binding them together, so that after a time she seemed to herself not to be moving from her own volition. As if something else—the music, perhaps—created the dance, using their bodies.

A singeing heat tingled on her skin when he touched her. His hand moved against her bare back, and she felt a shivering response all down her spine. He bent his head to murmur something, and even his breath against her neck caused a delicious melting in her, and her blood flowed with warm sweetness like the taste of honey.

Then he dropped his hands and stood a little away from her, and she knew she had been wrong about the bonds that linked them. They were not the product of the music, but something else. Because they were still there, strong and vibrant, and binding her to him, when the music stopped.

Fifteen

She was a hit, a very palpable hit. A tiny, perfect princess, a survivor from hell who had kept her humour, her truth…and her predilection for straight talk and plain, pungent language, which after months of tutoring no one had quite been able to eradicate in her. The world loved what it saw and wanted more.

After that interview, as Gazi had predicted, the demand for appearances by the Bagestani princess and her rescuer went nuclear, and the Gulf Island campaign was to be stepped up and taken all over the world.

"We'll need some support," Gazi insisted. "We don't want anyone getting burn-out, and Shakira is new to all this."

So other members of the royal family were drafted, and Farida, too. "A B-list celebrity," Noor said with a grin one day, overhearing Gazi on his mobile with a chat show producer who wanted Shakira and Sharif and was being offered Noor and Farida and Jamila instead. "Just what I always dreamed of."

Gazi hung up and shook his head. "You're not B-list, Princess. It's just that they hadn't realized yet that you're on offer.

What a blessing you were so reclusive when you got back from your adventure with Bari! Believe me, they jumped at the chance to get the heiress who bolted from her wedding and spent her honeymoon with her fiancé on a desert island."

"I did not bolt from my wedding," Noor denied primly. "Bari's grandfather withdrew his permission."

He grinned. "That's the ticket, Princess."

It seemed strange to her that she should have discovered love, real love, not with her family, not for the Sultan or even her grandmother, but for Sharif. She had believed that she loved her family, because she wanted to love them. But when her heart opened for Sharif she learned that love was very different from a feeling of wanting to love. And now she loved not just Sharif, but her family, too.

It was mysterious, inexplicable, but something had happened when he told her her name—earlier, even, for when she stole his wallet, hadn't she been half glad then that he had come after her? But she hadn't begun to understand herself until that night she had danced with him, and felt how her heart cleaved to his.

Her heart had been closed before Sharif. But every moment she was with him, it opened a little more. *Like a dark, locked room,* she told herself. *And he unlocked the door and came in with a light, and looked at things that no one has ever seen.*

But he hadn't seen everything, she reminded herself anxiously. Now she knew what love really was—but would Sharif love her, if he knew?

What the family called in private *The Al Jawadi Islands-for-the-Islanders Road Show* went from success to raging success. They were capturing the public imagination. Between the Princesses, the Cup Companions, and the islanders themselves, as represented by Farida and her daughter, the campaign caught fire. Someone started selling T-shirts over the Internet, and sent a dozen samples to the palace.

"Why not?" said Gazi, and on the next chat show Noor, Farida and Jamila had *People Need Sanctuary Too* emblazoned on their chests. After that the T-shirts began appearing on the streets.

It had been Gazi's idea that Noor and Farida would make a good team, since Noor had been shipwrecked on the island, Solomon's Foot, where Farida's family had lived for generations. On the practical front, Noor could translate when Farida was interviewed in English. On the bums-on-seats front, as Gazi put it, Farida and Jamila pulled the heartstrings, and Noor added the glitter.

"Shakira, of course, does both," Gazi confided to Sharif. "Her kind are few and far between, Sharif. She's one of a kind, and they're all after her."

The two Cup Companions looked at each other.

"Do you think I don't know that?"

"What do they say? 'You'd better hurry, 'cause it's going fast.'"

"Over my dead body." Sharif showed his teeth.

Gazi's hands went up. "Okay, okay. So long as you're on the case. A person would have to be blind not to know how you feel, and the way she looks at you, you're miles ahead of the rest of the field. But are you making your advantage good?"

"She's unique, Gazi, as you say. She looks great—sometimes you'd swear she'd recovered as if it all had never happened. But underneath Princess Shakira is still Hani half the time, an urchin fighting the world for the right to live. She needs room to find herself a little more before I start labelling her as mine. She's got a right to discover herself."

It was killing him to wait, but he knew he was right. And giving Shakira time didn't mean giving anyone else a chance. He could keep the others away.

Farida's husband was found, in a prison far from the capital, where the prison superintendent had destroyed the prison records before fleeing. Hashim Sabzi was thin, weak and ill, but at least he had not been tortured. The prison superintendent, a far-seeing man, had noted the direction of the wind a couple of years before the Return, and tailored his activities accordingly.

Hashim moved to the palace to be with Farida, where he was under medical observation. He wasn't well enough to make the next talk show appearance with his family, as the producer had hoped.

But Farida and Jamila went, as scheduled.

What happened was completely unexpected. It was Noor's own idea to take along the doll she had found under the burnt house on Solomon's Foot, the doll she had given the name *Laqiya,* the foundling. Gazi had given the idea the thumbs-up, telling her to bring the doll out if the moment was good. But no one had mentioned it to Farida.

"Tell us what you ate, Princess, because I think that's what most people worry about—did you have to eat grubs while you were shipwrecked?"

Noor laughed. "No, but it was a close-run thing! We survived on turtles' eggs and fish and what we could forage in the forest," she said. "Then we found the tragic remains of the village. Farida's village, I know now. The houses had all been burnt, but even so there was some useful material for the shelter we were building. And it was great to find some self-seeded vegetables in the abandoned gardens."

"So you—"

"And there was one more thing I found, and I think this speaks louder than anything for the unspeakable nature of what Ghasib and Mystery Resorts committed on those islands," Noor went on. "I brought it today and I'd like to show it to you."

"Of course."

Noor bent down to the smart carryall she had brought with her, lifted out a plastic bag, and opened it.

"As long as I live, I will never forget the day I found this, in the ruins of a wrecked, half-burnt house. For me, this little doll said it all."

She drew Laqiya out of the plastic shroud and sat the little rag doll on her knee. "To me this doll is a symbol of—"

A piercing shriek electrified them all.

"*Aminaaaaaa!*" screamed Jamila, and then, "Mama, it's my Amina!" and she launched herself off her mother's lap to run to Noor, wrapped her hands around the doll, tore it from Noor's startled grasp, and danced around the studio, the doll hugged to a cheek wet with tears.

Then she turned to her mother with an expression that had the studio audience groping for their own hankies.

"We have Baba and Amina, Mama. Can we go home now?"

"Dear Princess Shakira," read the note.

I have seen you on television. What has happened to you and the Gulf Islanders is dreadful, but it has been very difficult to know what to do. When I saw that little girl, I knew I couldn't remain silent. They call it "corporate secrets," but I can't square it with my conscience any longer.

It's all eyewash. They never wanted to turn those islands into a resort—that was just the excuse they gave for getting rid of the islanders. What they want is exclusive patents on the healing herbs that the islanders use in their traditional medicine. Those herbs have been proven effective in clinical studies. Webson Attary Pharmaceuticals have got scientists working on synthesizing six different herbs, so they can patent the formulae.

But that means stopping the island trade in the natural herbs. And the legal side is complicated, because some drug companies are getting slapped with lawsuits for things like that. Who knows where the judgement of the International Court will go in a few years? And because the herbs are unique to the islands, it might mean having to pay the islanders big royalties down the road.

That's what it's all about—ensuring the future profits of Webson Attary Pharmaceuticals. And it could be very big—one of the herbs that the islanders use to heal burns and abrasions looks like having important skin rejuvenation properties. It's got a very expensive future as an ingredient in anti-aging cream.

You'll get everything you need from the document attached. It's top secret—no one's supposed to have a copy. It's all in there. There's a lot of technical language. Among other things it says that the turtles are indeed unique to the islands, and technically they could be called "endangered" because of the high risk of their small numbers and having only one known habitat. But that's not a situation human beings have created. In fact, there has been no significant decrease in their numbers over the past fifty years. So the islanders are not a problem.

I'm sorry I can't sign this. I hope I meet you one day and can signal to you, so you'll know who I am.

They walked in the garden at night, his arm around her, her head against his heart. Around them the fountains burbled and sang, and the scent of sleepy roses perfumed the air.

"It couldn't have happened without you," Sharif said. "Congratulations, Princess. Not everyone can turn life's hard experiences around and make something so positive out of them."

"Does Ashraf say the islanders will be able to go home now?"

"Yes, this has changed everything. The original contract for the lease of the islands wasn't signed in good faith, which means the company won't be able to ask the courts to enforce it. But in any case the fallout from public opinion if the company now proceeded with a claim is too big to risk."

Shakira smiled and sighed.

"This also means we'll have an easier time with the tribal council. Now that we're no longer fighting for their agreement to resettle the islanders inland we'll make headway on other issues."

She lifted her head and looked up into his face. "It's all because of you. So many lives changed so completely, because you found me in that camp. Especially my life."

He was silent for a long breath. Then he murmured, "My life, too, Princess."

Nervously she withdrew, but his arm held her firm, and she subsided against his heart again. "I love you, Shakira," he said softly.

Her blood created a flurry in her breast. "Do you?" she whispered. "Do you *love* me?" Tears spurted over her cheeks, as if being loved by him were too much for her heart to bear. "Oh, Sharif!"

He turned to face her, wrapping his arms around her as the night embraced the moon. "Very, very much. I want you to be my wife. Will you?"

"Oh!" Her breath caught, and she swallowed over the lump that had suddenly leapt into her throat. "Oh, Sharif! I don't think—oh, *Allah,* marry? How could I be married? I'm not like Noor, or even Jalia. I'm not a woman, I'm still half a boy. You know that better than anyone. I'm so ignorant about everything. I need to go to school, and I need—oh, how can I be a wife?"

"Do you love me, Shakira?"

His voice was half rough, half gentle, and her skin shivered with the danger that beckoned. "Yes—oh, *yes,* I do! But—"

He bent his head and his mouth came closer and closer while her heart kicked and struggled. Tenderly, he brushed her lips with his, and a kind of sweetness she had never tasted before flowered in her, as if her heart tasted the scent of roses.

He lifted his mouth a little away, and rested his forehead against hers. "If you love me, the rest can wait, Shakira. We can take it as slowly as you need. But tell me you love me."

It was the first time in her life that anyone had asked for her love, and her heart cracked with the sweet pain and the newness of it. To be someone whose love was valued—oh, how far she had come from Burry Hill!

"Is it—is it important to you?" she pressed, just to prolong the sweetness.

"Nothing has ever been as important."

She could not hold out longer against that. "I love you, Sharif. I don't think I knew what love was before I loved you. But it's—it's when your heart opens, isn't it? When someone gets inside your heart and you're glad they're there."

"Yes," he said, for he, too, had learned that frightening joy. "Yes, that's what love is."

"And then you find that there's room for lots more people, too. I—I thought I loved my family, but my heart didn't know how to open right away. And then you went in and now—now I can love everyone I want to love."

His arms wrapped her so tightly then that she couldn't breathe, but it seemed you didn't need breath when you had love. His mouth sought hers again, but although she lifted her lips he sensed her fear, and again, though he trembled with the effort, his lips only brushed hers.

"Promise to be my wife," he whispered.

"But I'm so—I told you why."

"Shakira, you are perfect and true. What is it you fear?"

"I don't know," she whispered helplessly, for how could she tell him?

He looked at her closely, as if he guessed something, and she dropped her eyes.

"Let's sit down," Sharif said after a moment. He led her to a bench under a rustling tree, and they sat. Above them the bright moon sailed above a wisp of grey cloud in the lush, purple-black sky. Its light gleamed on the turquoise dome, and on the sparkling fountain.

"I want to tell you a story," he said.

"I love your stories. Who is it about?" she demanded. In the distance she heard music, and her grandmother's voice.

When the incense does not burn
It gives off no perfume
Only those who have been consumed by love
Understand me....

"It's about you, Shakira, as all good stories are," Sharif said. "Listen."

Sixteen

"**O**nce upon a time," he began, and with a sigh she nestled against his side. "Once upon a time, there was a young man named Yunus. He worked hard and saved his money, and one day he decided that it was time for him to marry.

"Now, Yunus had several times seen a pretty girl at his neighbour's window, and he thought that she would make him a fine wife. So he went to his neighbour, and asked him for the girl's hand in marriage.

"But the neighbour looked gloomy. 'Yes, it is time my Fatima was married,' he said, 'but I would not inflict her on you, Yunus, good friend that you are. For although she is lovely to look on, she has the voice of a corncrake, and a very bad temper with it. There is only one thing which can be done to correct this, and it is far too difficult for me to suggest that you attempt it. No one should go to so much trouble for my little Fatima.'

"But Yunus was undaunted, and he asked what could be done. 'I have been told by a wise man,' said the neighbour, 'that three drops of water from the Well of Sweetness, carried in a tiny bottle, will cure her bad temper.'

"'Then I will go and get the water,' Yunus declared. 'Where is the Well of Sweetness?'

"'The woman who sleeps on the steps of the mosque knows where it is,' said the neighbour. 'But let me urge you not to go to so much trouble, my friend!'

"But Yunus was determined and, having first purchased a tiny bottle in the bazaar, he approached the beggar on the steps of the mosque. He dropped a gold coin in her bowl, and then asked her how he could find the Well of Sweetness.

"'Travel seven days to the west, and seven to the east,' she said. 'There you will find a river. Cross that, and you will come to where a Giant lives. Ask the Giant what you want to know.'

"Yunus followed her directions until he came to the river. As the ferryman rowed him across, he asked about the Giant, and learned that the Giant lived in a cave in the mountains. 'But be polite, or he will kill you with his club,' advised the ferryman.

"Yunus walked a long, weary way, and at last met the Giant. Politely wishing him peace, he explained his mission. 'Since you have spoken so respectfully to me, I will tell you,' said the Giant, 'though few who come this way are so polite, and I usually kill them. Inside my cave is a secret passage, guarded by a three-headed dragon. When you see him, say, *By leave of Suleiman, Son of David, upon whom be peace, let me pass!* And the dragon will let you pass.'

"All was as the Giant had foretold, and after passing the dragon, Yunus travelled far along the dark passage. Finally there was a shaft of light ahead, and he saw a beautiful fairy pulling up a bucket of water from a deep well. 'Peace be upon you!' Yunus cried, and the fairy replied, 'And upon you, peace, mortal! Come, and I will fill your bottle.' And she put three drops of water into the little bottle and gave it back to him.

"Then he went back along the passage, and it seemed a longer and harder way to him than before, with the darkness cloying and stones cutting his feet. But finally he reached the dragon, recited the magic sentence, and was again allowed to pass.

"When he reached the Giant's cave again, he showed him the bottle of water from the Well of Sweetness, and the Giant commended him. 'Now, mortal,' he said, 'you must work for me a year and a day, and then you may go home.'

"So Yunus served the Giant for a year and a day, tending and milking his goats and cooking the Giant's meals. He washed his dishes and scrubbed his shirts and spread them to dry on bushes, and he kept the fire alight. And at the end of a year and a day, the Giant was so pleased with his work that he gave him a bag of gold and sent him on his way.

"When he returned home, Yunus was greeted by his neighbour. 'You have been so long away, friend!' exclaimed the man. 'We were afraid for you. What an experience you must have had! Did you get the water from the Well of Sweetness?'

"Yunus told him of his adventures, gave him the bottle of magic water to give to Fatima, and went home to prepare himself for the wedding. When all the arrangements were complete, his bride appeared, veiled and magnificently dressed, and the celebrations began. Yunus felt he was the happiest man alive.

"That night, when the feasting was over, Yunus removed Fatima's veil, and found her to be as beautiful as he could wish. Her voice was sweet and soft as the cooing of a dove. 'Dear wife,' he said, 'what wonders there are in the world, *Al-hamdolillah!* How glad I am, hearing your soft voice, that I went to the Well of Sweetness for your sake!'

"'What do you mean, husband?' his bride asked. And Yunus explained that her father had sent him to get the magic water to soften her voice and improve her temper.

"At this Fatima threw back her head and laughed and laughed. 'It was not I who had the bad temper, husband, but my mother! My father was told by a wise man that three drops of water from the Well of Sweetness on her tongue would transform her. And so he made up his mind that whoever asked for me in marriage should be made to go for the water.'

"Yunus laughed with her, and he and his wife were so happy together that they never had a cross word all their lives."

Shakira sat in silence while he waited and watched. "That's about me?" she asked at last. "I don't understand."

"Don't you see that Yunus has seen perfection and loves it, but because of some flaw in himself, some doubt, he imagines that his future bride is flawed? It may be that Yunus has to go on a quest, but his travails and his search do not affect his bride. They affect Yunus, so that in the end he is brought to a state where he is able to appreciate what Fatima is. That is the true end of most quests, isn't it?"

"But who am I in the story? Yunus or Fatima?"

"You are both, aren't you?" Sharif said.

"Both?"

"And perhaps everyone else also. Fatima is your true inner self, Shakira. The doubting part of you thinks that she is flawed, but she is perfectly beautiful and true. It may be that your outer self has to be brought to a state where you can recognize your own truth, but your inner self needs no transformation."

She sat silent, taking it in. Was it true? Was the fear that she felt just that—fear? She hardly knew what she was afraid of. Of not being good enough. Of still being too close to the boy who had learned to think himself worthless, unlovable.

She was afraid of being judged.

4
The Beloved

The Dream of the Beloved

In the dream she swam in a jade-and-emerald sea, cool and sweet and spangled with gold, and he was beside her. Naked she swam, and the water held her close as a lover, so that with every wave that lapped, a delicious pleasure rippled across her skin.

Then it was not the water that held her, but his body, for he lay under her like a bed, and now his hands and the waves caressed her together.

In the dream he kissed her, and her heart sounded her yearning, and her delight. In the dream she had no fear as his hands cupped her cheeks, her head, and held her face to the sweet whisper of his mouth on her flesh. His lips brushed her eyelids, the bridge of her nose, her cheek, her ear, and her blood pulsed eagerly up under the caress, seeking his warmth, and then rushing to carry it to every part of her being.

In the dream her body melted into his with a divine and fearless hunger, and she yearned against him, so that he felt her trust and her love as one thing. His arms encircled her with fierce and tender passion, and his hand cupped her head and drew her up to his wildly seeking kiss. And only then did she understand how long he had waited for her, and how hungrily.

His face was shadowed in the dream, but she knew he smiled. His eyes were dark and as deep as the sea, and in them she saw a glow. The glow reached deep into her heart, and she felt its touch all through her being.

"It's love!" she exclaimed.

"Yes," he said, though she could not hear his voice.

Was it his hands, or was it the sea, that began to stroke her then, so that joy and love and melting pleasure pulsed through her? She sighed and moaned, and stretched herself luxuriously against his body the sea, and felt his touch everywhere.

She clasped him tight, and then she knew that he was herself, and she was him, that they were one being, and one with the sea. Then the joy was urgent in her, like a storm, pressing up through soul and heart and body, seeking a way to the sea.

Pleasure beat unmercifully against their bodies. It drew her down into the green depths. Deep she went, and deeper, amongst spangles of golden light. The water, or his hands, stroked and loved her, for he stayed at her side as she sank, and the pleasure pushed and pushed in her.

Deep within the mysterious green then she saw that they were among shining domes and minarets. And as they moved under arches and between rows of pillars, she saw a golden pavilion encased in a golden glow.

Inside the pavilion there were chests of jewels, red and green and blue and white, yellow and turquoise, purple and black. And there were treasures of gold and silver. And all the jewels and treasures were her own.

"Oh!" she cried. "I didn't know this!"

He turned to her, and wrapped her again, and then at last the beating, pushing pleasure found its way. It flooded up and coursed through them, and over them, and made its way out *into the endless green sea. Then she swam in the sea of pleasure, and was part of it.*

And then came love, a deep, flooding love that filled her, heart and body and soul, with calm and knowing.

Her heart lifted and soared, and they followed it up till they floated on the surface of the green, green sea, and the night sky sparked and spangled all around them.

Seventeen

For the next two days she could think of nothing but Sharif. His eyes, the way they had looked at her, flames of moonlight and passion in their depths—the memory of it trembled in her bones. As if she was precious and he was frightened to the soul that she might not love him.

She did love him. Oh, she loved him! She couldn't prevent herself loving him, though she knew how dangerous it was to love. How fragile existence was.

But she could not give him the answer he wanted.

She did not see him often, because the tribal leaders were in the palace and Sharif was sitting in on the negotiations. For the second day she ate lunch with Noor and Jalia, who were now full of their wedding plans, having dress fittings with Kamila and discussing music and the guest list replies and a host of other things.

"Whose bridesmaid am I going to be?" Shakira asked when they showed her the fabulous designs for the bridesmaids' cos-

tumes. As tradition dictated, each would wear a different outfit, from a choice of beautiful colours.

"At the moment, we think we won't have separate groups.
It'll just be a flock of gorgeous girls doing duty for both of
us. But we can't be certain yet. Maybe we'll have to split them
into two groups."

It was exciting, but of course not nearly so thrilling for Shakira as for the two brides. Especially not when she was desperate to see Sharif again.

When they did meet, it was a snatched half hour in the private courtyard that evening, where they walked alone.

He did not press her for an answer. She was so relieved by
this that she scarcely noticed that whatever he said seemed to
take for granted that they would be together forever.

"Now that the issue of the island resettlement is resolved,
the islanders become the Sultana's concern, since refugees fall
under her purview," Sharif said. "I told Dana I'd like to in-
volve myself with it. She has asked me to take charge of repatriation—not just of the islanders, but all refugees."

She gazed at him. "Oh! Will you—will you like that work?"

He looked into her eyes. "It is very close to my heart. I want
to prevent anyone spending one day more than absolutely
necessary in the hell where I found you, my beloved."

Her heart thumped painfully. "Oh—!"

"We both wondered if you would like to work with me on
the project."

"Oh!" she said, in a different voice. "Oh, yes! Why didn't
I think of that? Will we be able to bring them all home?"

"First on the agenda has to be finding temporary accommodation for them. Ash has been putting a new proposal to
the tribal council—there's no longer the necessity to ask for
permanent resettlement of the islanders, but still we need
space to house everyone while they are assessed and their
homes are rebuilt. Of course no one wants another refugee
camp, but it seems better to bring them home, even if we
haven't yet got permanent accommodation for them. Ash has

a powerful ally on the tribal council, Tabasi's son, who has a big impact for such a young man. His influence over his father is very strong, we hear, and where Tabasi goes, the council goes. We'll probably reach an agreement tomorrow that will allow us to put up temporary accommodation for a certain number only. That still leaves a sizable number…."

"Can't we house some in Ghasib's New Palace?" Shakira suggested. "It's ugly, but not nearly as ugly as Burry Hill, and it's huge, and it's got plumbing! And at least it's already built. It's not doing anything at the moment, is it? Waiting to be turned into a tourist site or a hotel complex if Ash can find investors!" She snorted. "Why not do something useful with it?"

Sharif threw back his head and laughed the laugh of a man who has suddenly been shown the answer that's been staring everyone in the face.

The next day was Friday, and the Sultan hosted a dinner at the palace for the tribal council. It was not a public occasion, only family and Cup Companions dining with the tribal leaders in the formal dining room off the Sultan's Anteroom, where visiting monarchs and heads of state were entertained.

They were a fierce-looking group, most wearing the flowing kaftans and hooded burnouses more common in the desert than the cities, some in the baggy trousers and vests of the mountain tribes. All men, for the tribes hadn't yet admitted women into the council.

Shakira had met such men in the camps, for the tribes had often been seen as a danger by Ghasib, and she instinctively felt comfortable with them. But she was slipping into her easy, man-to-man Hani ways, and since she was a beautiful and beautifully dressed woman, not all the men were so comfortable with her as she was with them.

Sharif appeared in the doorway, his eyes searching the room. His gaze fell on her, and she was surprised to note a frown in his gaze before he saw that she had seen him, and changed it to a smile.

He did not come to her, but as she watched made his way towards where the Sultan and Sultana were standing, under the great portrait of Hafzuddin. Shakira watched as he bowed and spoke, and then, to her surprise, the Sultana looked her way, the same frown of concern on her face, and started across the room towards her.

At that moment her attention was caught by something at the door, and she turned to see that a man was standing in the doorway, his fierce black eyes combing the room.

He was a man much younger than most of the others, but he carried himself with the same authority as the greybeards. Shakira felt a glimmer of recognition. Perhaps she had met him in one of the camps? He was in tribal dress, wearing a voluminous white burnous open over his shoulders like a cape, a dark waistcoat, the traditional flowing *shalwar kamees,* and a navy turban with the ends falling over his shoulder.

"Who is that man?" she asked Jalia's fiancé, who was standing near with Jalia. Latif Abd al Razzaq lifted his head.

"That's old Tabasi's son. He's been Ash's strong supporter on the council, and we're assuming it's his influence over the old man that has convinced them at last."

The man was sternly handsome, his skin darkly bronzed by the sun, and he looked strong, proud, and every inch a tribal sheikh. His eyes raked the gathering with an eagle's ferocity.

Suddenly his gaze lighted on her. Something like recognition buzzed in her, and Shakira shivered as the man, his burnous billowing around him, started across the room towards her.

"Wow, that's some hunk!" Noor whispered in her ear. "And it looks as though he might be going to give Sharif a run for his money! Sharif isn't happy about it, either, by what I see!"

Sharif was crossing the room towards the man at an angle to cut him off, and Shakira had never seen him move so fast, practically pushing people out of his way.

He reached Tabasi's son a few yards away from where Shakira stood, and she heard an urgent, low-voiced murmur. But the tribal leader flung up a haughty hand and pushed past the Cup Companion. In another moment he was face-to-face with her.

"Shakira," Dana's voice spoke behind her. "Prepare yourself for—"

The man stood gazing at her for an electric moment, an expression in his eyes that almost frightened her. She heard a rushing sound in her ears, and the light went dark for a moment, as though she had made some discovery that hadn't yet reached consciousness.

Then Sharif said, "Shakira, this is Sheikh Mazin ibn Tabasi al Johari." She had never seen him look so anxious, as if he did not know how to handle the situation. "The Sheikh believes—you must understand we have no proof yet, but—"

But Sheikh Mazin ibn Tabasi al Johari was impatient of this preparation. His hands reached out to grip her shoulders, and she gasped at the urgency of his grasp.

"*Sister,*" he said simply. "My sister Shakira. It is a great happiness to find you."

The word ricocheted around the room as once the sound of her name had done, wildly, crazily, like a trapped bird seeking escape, and her heart fluttered in time with its wings.

Sister. A dozen whispers behind her in the room repeated the astonishing, amazing word.

"Sister?" Her own voice croaked as she pronounced it, the wonderful, marvellous word she had waited to hear for fifteen long, hungry years. "Are you my brother? Oh, are you my *brother?* Are you really…Mazin?"

"Shakira, we need evidence before—" she heard someone, the Sultana perhaps, begin, but she was gazing up into that dark face, hungrily searching for the brother she knew.

His eyes glittered with unshed tears as he gazed down at her, and his mouth split in a smile, revealing strong white teeth. One eyetooth stood proud of the others, a little twisted over its neighbour.

"Mazin!" she cried, with a voice that shivered down the spine of everyone present and caused the precious piece of glass on a nearby table to ring. "Mazin! It is you! Oh, it is you, my brother!"

She flung herself into his arms, and he held her as tightly as she had always dreamed, and his tears fell and mingled with hers.

They walked and talked in the garden for hours, searching for mutual landmarks in their fifteen years of unshared history.

"Oh, when you were doing that, I was there or there," she would say, and he would say, "Ah, when we heard that news I never thought—"

There was so much to say, so much to hear. She was hungry for every detail of her brother's life, and he for hers.

"Gulab gave me a pack and told me to go into the mountains the night after you were taken. He said I was no longer safe in the house. I am sure he was right. There were some in the village…"

"Oh, weren't you terrified? Going into the mountains in the dark, alone…"

Mazin only shook his head, a powerful warrior unwilling to recall a time when he was vulnerable and afraid.

"I spent three days walking before I met a hunter. He took me to the fortress, where his sheikh was. It was Tabasi. He was already an old man, and his sons had all died in a terrible epidemic that had swept the tribe—some said deliberately sent by Ghasib. Tabasi adopted me. I was not with strangers. My grandmother was a Johari herself, and the tribe knew my father's name and had a bond of kinship with us. I never suffered as you suffered, Sister. If I went hungry, we all went hungry. In the drought we lost many."

She told him of her life—the Bahramis; England; the bombing; the camps; and he listened closely, as if to know her by what she had suffered. He listened in silence, nodding, turning his head from time to time to look down at his sister in the moonlight.

And then, because he was her brother, she had the courage to tell it all.

"Now you have told me," she heard at the end. "I am your brother, your guardian. These memories will not trouble you anymore," Mazin said, with his uncomplicated mountain wisdom.

"And now, there is my friend Sharif Azad al Dauleh," said Mazin.

She breathed a silent gasp.

It was late, they didn't know how late, but the moon had climbed high, and the sky behind had changed from purple-black to midnight.

"I have met him much during our negotiations. And I have seen how he looks at you, heard his voice pronounce your name. He wants to make all right for you, is that not so?"

"Yes," whispered Shakira.

"He asks you to be his wife."

She nodded. "But I—I don't—I'm not—"

He looked at her closely. "He is a noble man, Sister. He has been honoured by the Sultan, and he is of a good family, whose tribe has always been on good terms with al Johari. You have my permission to marry Sharif Azad al Dauleh."

"Mazin, he—I—do you think he really loves me enough for that? Won't he—if he knew—?"

Mazin frowned. "He is a *man,* Sister." Her brother invested the word with a deeper meaning than she had ever heard it given. "Does a man want a woman only for her beauty, or for everything she is and has been?"

And somehow, just like that, she could see her way.

Eighteen

"**D**id you know who he was all along?"

"It never crossed my mind. He doesn't seem to have the al Jawadi look," Sharif assured her, "and for once I wasn't looking for it."

"A little," she said. "When he is laughing hard."

"I am glad you laughed with your brother, Shakira," he commented softly. "There wasn't much laughing going on in our meetings. No, it was almost chance that I asked him, and not some other member of the council, whether he had ever heard of a boy found wandering the mountains. As we spoke he got more and more agitated, and finally he asked your father's name. When he heard it, nothing could stop him."

They were wandering in the garden at night, always her favourite time in the garden, when the scent of roses seemed sweetest on the night air.

She rested her head where it belonged, against his heart, and they walked in silence while the moon climbed the night sky.

"In the way of the tribes, your brother has agreed to our marriage, Shakira," he said softly.

"I have to tell you something, Sharif," she interrupted hurriedly. "If you—if you still want to marry me when I've said it, then…then I will."

He went still for a moment. "There is nothing you can tell me that will make me change my mind about wanting you for my wife."

"I have to tell you."

Seeing the intensity in her face, he nodded once, and fell silent.

"There was—it was in the first camp, in Parvan. There was a man there—everyone knew he was a Kaljuk, because of the way he pronounced certain words, but he didn't seem to realize that. He was married to a Parvani woman and had been living in Parvan for years, and he seemed to think no one knew.

"He was a bad man. And he always picked on the weakest people. He stole food from pregnant women."

Sharif muttered something.

"Everyone knew or suspected he was attacking women, but he chose women—girls—who were alone, with no husbands or brothers to avenge them, and so nothing ever got done. And afterwards the women would always keep quiet out of shame."

Sharif closed his eyes and breathed deep. "You were alone," he said. "With no one to avenge you."

"I was about twelve. It was just before my stepmother was killed. I'd been a girl again ever since England, you know, but I was still—I hadn't gone through puberty, so I didn't really think—I wasn't afraid of him, the way some were. But one day…"

He let her pause, struggling with the anger that rose in him, the murderous rage and outrage that would have ripped the villain apart if he had faced him.

A cloud obscured the moon, hiding his face from her.

"I told you the Kaljuk planes used to bomb and strafe the camp sometimes as if it were a game to them. They would chase someone with strafing, and sometimes kill them and sometimes not. When we heard the Kaljuk planes, we used to all run to the kitchen building."

"Yes," he said, for she had told him this part of the story before.

Shakira took a deep breath. "One day I was in the school tent. We only had a few textbooks, and they were always kept at the school. And that day I was there by myself, studying, and I didn't hear the planes. I got up to sharpen my pencil with the knife from the supplies box, and that's when I realized the planes were coming. I ran to the door. Almost everyone was already inside the kitchen hut, and the planes were close, and I didn't know whether to run or not. I was—" Even now the fear was almost overwhelming, and he put his arm around her to remind her of where she was. "I was so scared."

Her eyes were dark. "Someone came around the corner of the school tent as I stood there, and it was him. The Kaljuk. He glanced over at me, and I saw his face change…he turned and came towards me. And then…I would have run then, though the first planes were almost on us, but he grabbed me and shoved me back inside the school before I—before I…"

She sobbed once, but her eyes were dry as she stared into the past.

"Shakira, I love you," Sharif said.

"I'd been sharpening the pencil, and I—he dragged me towards the teacher's table and started pushing me down and I…I…" She took a deep, shuddering breath and looked straight into his eyes.

"I still had the knife in my hand," she said baldly.

It was the first moment he allowed himself to breathe.

She wiped her eyes convulsively.

"I stabbed him. I don't know where it hit, I just remember lifting my arm and—I hated him, and I hit him as hard as I could."

Her eyes left his and sought the past again. "There was blood…suddenly it gushed out everywhere. He grunted and I shoved him, and he went down on the ground. I ran outside. The blood was on my hands, and the planes were screaming right overhead, very low. I was sure they were going to strafe me." Her eyes were black and bleak.

"I can never forget that—running to the kitchens with that man's blood on my hands, and the planes…and then the bombs started falling."

He was weeping with relief, with anger, with emotions stronger than anything he had ever felt in his life.

"His body was found, and no one ever questioned what killed him. I think some of the men—just the way they looked at each other when his body was found made me think they knew that it wasn't the bombs. One man said, *It is God's justice*. And there were so many casualties that day that the body was never examined."

She looked up then, for his judgement.

"Do you tell me you felt one moment's guilt over this man's death?" Sharif demanded.

"No," she whispered. "I can't feel guilty, even—even if I did kill him. That's why I had to tell you, Sharif. I wasn't sorry—I'm *not* sorry!—for what I did. And maybe that—makes me as bad as he was. He was bad, an evil man. Women cheered and spat on his body when it was found. And I was *glad* I had done it, because he couldn't hurt anybody else."

"I am glad too, Beloved," he said softly.

He drew her against his side, and she sighed from the depths of her being, and they walked a little.

"And was it then that you became Hani again?"

She gave a half laugh, though she knew she should never be surprised by his understanding. "Yes. A week later the kitchen was bombed and my stepmother died. The camp was—we were moved after that, and it was easy to say I was a boy."

"And later, your protection extended to other women and girls—like Farida and Jamila. That is why you adopted them."

She blinked. "I—I suppose so."

"My brave and courageous Hani. And what did you fear from me, Beloved? Did you think that I could judge differently in such a case? Could you imagine that I would say what you did was wrong?"

"I—I didn't know. I just knew I had to tell you. But I couldn't. And then…I told Mazin."

He stopped then, and drew her into his arms, and she rested her head against its natural home. It beat strongly, reassuringly, under her ear. Above, the moon sailed serenely free of the cloud that had hidden its face, and glinted off the pool, the tumbling fountain, and the great golden dome in the distance.

"And this is what kept you from me," he said after a long silence in which their hearts spoke without words. "But now you will not be kept from me any longer. Now you will be my wife. I love you, Shakira. In my heart you are my wife already. Tell me that it is so for you, too."

"Yes," she breathed, and the last weight lifted from her heart, and like the moon, it soared free.

Nineteen

ISLANDERS TO GO HOME

Bagestan will begin the repatriation of the Gulf Island refugees this week, it was announced today. The refugees were kept waiting in refugee camps around the world while the situation of the Aswad turtle was resolved. The islanders' cause had been taken up by Princess Shakira of Bagestan, herself a long-time refugee. The Princess is reported to be delighted by the news.

"**W**ell, Marta, it's another royal wedding in Bagestan," said Barry. "We seem to be making a habit of this."

"Yes, and a fabulous *triple* wedding, too, Barry! We haven't seen one of those since the handsome Princes of Barakat all were lost to panting womanhood in one day."

"I don't think you ever recovered from the blow."

"Well, it's your turn to suffer now! Three princesses of the al Jawadi family agreed to exchange their vows—in one joint ceremony—with three of the handsomest Cup Companions out there, and believe me, that is saying something!"

"Tell us about the princesses, Marta."

"Well. They're all direct descendants of the old Sultan of Bagestan, Hafzuddin al Jawadi, Barry, but none of them knew it until after the bloodless coup we in the West call the Silk Revolution, but in Bagestan people mostly call the Return. Because, as you know, the royal family was in mortal danger from Ghasib's assassins for years, and had to flee to other countries and live under assumed names until the Sultan's grandson regained the throne.

"Princess Noor you'll remember because she hit the headlines a few months ago. She fled from her own wedding minutes before the vows were exchanged, provoking delicious speculation. Then she and her fiancé disappeared, and we had the terrible discovery that his plane was missing in a thunderstorm. Nearly everybody assumed the worst, but Princess Noor and Bari al Khalid were finally found shipwrecked on one of the deserted Gulf Islands. It was revealed that the reason for her flight was her fiancé's grandfather's eleventh-hour withdrawal of his permission for the marriage. Reason—some ancient family feud. Bari al Khalid rejected his grandfather's orders to marry a woman from another family, and the old man threatened to disinherit him. But when he died shortly afterwards, his will revealed that he had not made good on his threat.

"Princess Noor has since returned to university to begin her studies in science and engineering, Barry, and says she wants to find new approaches to old problems in Bagestan."

"Oh, well, I wouldn't have stood a chance there anyway. Brainy women never go for me, Marta."

"Next up is Princess Jalia, and she's way out of your reach, Barry, because Jalia lectured in Arabic at a university in Scotland! She's resigned that post now, in order to stay in Bagestan, but once the dust has settled on the wedding, she'll be kept busy in her new role as one of the Sultana's Cup Companions, with some sort of mandate in higher education, we're told. The man marrying her today is tall, dark and moody Latif Abd al Razzaq Shahin, whose grandfather was also famously a Cup Companion to the old Sultan, as well as the tribal leader of Sey-Shahin Valley, where those fabulous purple carpets come from.

"And then there's everybody's darling, the lovely Princess Shakira, who has been charming us all with her courage and spirit. She has heroically overcome her dreadful experiences in refugee camps while on the run from Ghasib's killers, and has championed the cause of the Gulf Islanders. She practically single-handedly took on the greedy multinational whose name we won't mention in polite company, and she's winning. Shakira is also planning to return to her studies, because she says she missed out on too much of her education while in the camps. She's been on the—sorry, what? Oh! We're going to Bagestan now, with Andrea on the live feed."

She looked up at the monitor, where the reporter's face was pictured, surrounded by a crowd of cheering Bagestanis, in front of the glowing golden dome of the Shah Jawad Mosque.

"What's happening there, Andrea?"

"Well, as you know, Marta, Bagestan has some unique and colourful traditions that go back a very long way, and this is going to be a traditional Bagestani wedding times three. Each of the bridegrooms is coming to Jawad Palace in his own procession, and I'm standing in Shah Jawad Square in front of the mosque, where the three processions are finally meeting up. We've been watching their approach for the past half hour. The processions converged at the top of the square just a few minutes ago, and the three bridegrooms themselves are now riding together. They're just about to enter the square, escorted by the crowd of family, friends, street urchins, musicians and interested onlookers. You should have a view on your monitor now."

"Yes, we do, and oh, Andrea, they are heartbreakers! Was there ever anything so magnificent?"

Bari al Khalid, Latif Abd al Razzaq Shahin and Sharif Azad al Dauleh entered the square on magnificent horses—black, white, and bay—though the colours were not easy to detect under the bright caparisons that they bore. Bridles, reins and saddles were richly jewelled, and the stirrups gleamed.

The bridegrooms were even more richly adorned. Flowing white silk *shalwar kamees* were covered by the traditional bridegroom's sleeveless cloth-of-gold coat, whose long skirts, spread over the horses' rumps, glowed like the mosque's dome in the bright sunshine. Over his shoulders each wore ropes of lustrous pearls and jewels and the chain of office of Cup Companion, and around his hips a jewelled scimitar. On the head of each, a wide turban was intricately wound with pearls and gold.

"Did you ever see anything so utterly gorgeous?" Marta commented, as the crowd cheered.

"I can't hear you, Marta—the roar is absolutely deafening," Andrea shouted. "The bridegrooms are riding abreast now, and don't they look fabulous! They're moving down the square, a slow march to the palace. In addition to everyone else, they're accompanied by dozens of musicians playing every conceivable instrument, and by no means all in concert! People are very excited, and here's someone…what do you think of the wedding?" she asked a young smiling couple, holding out her mike.

"Yes, it's great, they are following the old traditions. It's good that people do this. Under Ghasib, you know, it wasn't so easy."

"When you get married, will you do the same?"

"Yes, of course. It's tradition of our people. It's how we do it."

"The palace gates seem to be closed, Andrea," Marta observed, as the procession reached the other end of the square.

"Yes, and they'll remain closed. Here's what's happening now, Marta. Each of the grooms will ring the bell in turn, the gates will open—the old bell-pull has been installed for the occasion…there's the gatekeeper now, Marta, and by tradition he'll refuse the bridegrooms entrance and close the gate again. Usually a bridegroom knocks and is turned away three times, but today they'll each ring just once. Then they'll shout and draw their swords, and at that show of force, they'll be allowed in—and there they go, inside. So that's it from me, in Shah Jawad Square."

"And now we'll go inside the Great Court, where the wedding ceremony will take place."

"After a certain amount of resistance on the part of the brides, I understand," said Barry.

Marta sighed. "You wouldn't catch me resisting."

"Maybe that's your problem, Marta. You don't play hard to get."

The Great Court was filled with bright-hued canopies and pennants fluttering in the soft breeze, and a milling crowd of guests dressed in gorgeous silks and satins in every colour of the rainbow. Gold and jewels glittered and flashed in the sunshine, and there was music, laughter, and the burble of a dozen fountains.

"It looks like a medieval fairground!" Marta declared breathlessly. "All we're missing is the jugglers."

Into the scene burst the bridegrooms, scimitars held high, their horses prancing and snorting, surrounded by cheering supporters who were now firing rifles into the sky; and at this invasion the brides' guests formed up into ranks and began to heckle the men.

"What do you want here?" the crowd shouted.

"We come for our brides!" shouted the bridegrooms and their followers.

"Does a man seek a bride with naked steel?"

After a pause for consultation with their followers, the bridegrooms sheathed their swords in the jewelled scabbards on their hips.

"What do you want here?" the crowd shouted again.

"We come for our brides!"

"Does a man seek a bride on horseback?" the bridespeople challenged.

The men consulted and then dismounted, and as their followers parted to form a way for them, the three handsome bridegrooms, their golden coats fluttering on the wind, strode forward.

"Bring us our brides!" they shouted ferociously, and the crowd of bridespeople fell back.

"Find your bride, if you know her!" they called jubilantly, and pointed.

Under a majestic archway, tiled in blue, turquoise and purple, etched with arabesques, curlicues and mysterious, flowing calligraphy, three long lines of women and girls emerged. All were dressed in the most luscious silk, satin and organza, in a rainbow of bright shades, like a Sultan's jewel chest. They came in ruby, emerald, turquoise, sapphire, topaz, diamond, rose quartz, amethyst, and lapis lazuli, all set in threads of gold and silver.

All were closely veiled, with a large square of beautifully embroidered silk falling over head and shoulders.

The brilliantly hued clusters of female shapes moved slowly under the arch and followed a broad tiled pathway strewn with rose petals to the centre of the Grand Court. There the three lines converged in a single, silent group and stopped, veils fluttering in the breeze.

"Find your bride!" the crowd challenged the men again.

"All the bridesmaids must be unmarried," Marta murmured softly, as the grooms ceremonially exchanged insults with the crowd. "And by tradition, a man is bound to marry whomever he chooses at this point."

"Sounds risky."

"It is, apparently, possible that a family might go all out to buy a particularly brilliant costume for a girl who was for some reason unmarriageable, in the hopes of confusing the bride-groom at this point. So it's tradition, too, that the rightful bride wears some favour on her veil—of which the groom has been secretly informed, of course—to be sure of being recognized."

"It says here," added Barry, "that a popular cautionary tale in Bagestan tells about a bridesmaid whom the bride secretly sends to the bridegroom on the eve of the wedding, to tell him what sign to look for. But the girl falls in love with the groom at first sight, and so she describes her own outfit as being the one the bride will wear. And at the wedding the groom chooses her and marries her, and then the veil comes off and he makes a great show of anger when he discovers he hasn't married the right bride. But on their wedding night, he tells the girl that he fell in love with her, too, when he saw her, and he knew who she was and what trick she had played when he chose her. And they lived in peace and harmony for all their days, according to the story, and Allah sent them many children."

In the bright courtyard, the bridegrooms now walked among the veiled maidens, challenging them. "Are you she whom I seek?" they asked the veiled girls at random. But the maidens only bowed their heads and made no sign.

"Now they'll pretend to be about to choose the wrong woman," Marta said quietly, "in an effort to flush out the real bride by her agitated reaction. The women are forbidden to make any sign at this point, but it's a propitious sign for the marriage if the groom finds his bride quickly. Because, they say, if a man is sensitive, he should be able…now what's happening? There's some disturbance, but I can't quite—oh, it seems as though one of the brides has broken with tradition and laid claim to her man…. Is that—yes, it must be Princess Shakira, because that's Sheikh Sharif Azad al Dauleh she's holding so ferociously. And is that her brother Mazin expostulating with her?—but he's laughing too hard….

"What a staggeringly beautiful outfit she's wearing! The most luscious sea-green and gold, and—Shakira's traditional boyish touch—trousers underneath a gorgeously embroidered tunic. Perhaps she took that story to heart, because she's certainly not going to run the risk of her groom making a mistake…. I don't know what's being said there, but everyone is now laughing uproariously, especially Sharif. The breach of tradition has been taken in good part, and I suppose it's no more than we have come to expect from the iconoclastic princess. And now the other two grooms have found their brides, and they'll each lead their chosen partner to one of the gold-topped canopies set up on the *talar,* and the actual wedding ceremony can begin."

Twenty

Late in the night, bride and bridegroom wandered by the sea, alone.

"Who lives here?" she asked, lifting her face as a wave splashed against an outcrop of rock and the breeze carried droplets of water to her lips.

"It is Prince Rafi's holiday villa."

"It's beautiful, isn't it?"

They paused and turned to gaze at the golden glow above.

The house, encircled by rock, sat above the tiny private bay where they stood, their feet lapped by the cooling water. It enclosed on three sides a large courtyard set with pomegranate trees. In the centre a beautiful circular pool inlaid with intricate patterns of mosaic tile shimmered green with underwater lights, so that the trees cast faint shadows in the gloom. At one side a gold-domed pavilion was invitingly lit with soft golden light, and music played. Her grandmother's voice enticed the night.

When the incense does not burn
It gives off no perfume
Only those who have been consumed by love
Understand me....

"What a long journey it's been!" Shakira marvelled. Her head rested against his heart, and the strong, steady beat under her ear seemed to match the music.

"A thousand miles. And worth every step," Sharif said.

She looked up into his face, her eyes brushed with moonlight, seeking reassurance for a heart that, even now, could not quite believe.

But he had the rest of his life to make it real for her, and that was a whole new journey, and he took the first step tonight. "Even though my heart had been assailed by all that I'd seen," he said, "somehow Hani struck me a deeper blow than anything I'd experienced before."

She smiled wisely. "Maybe because your resistance was so worn down already."

He kissed the upturned face. "I thought I was so touched because you had suffered such deprivation, and maybe because you were an al Jawadi. You trusted no one, and I wanted you to trust me."

She smiled, considering it. "That's love, I think. Wanting to be trusted."

"That's a very small part of love, Beloved," he assured her. "There is much more."

They moved up the beach towards the courtyard, and her heart began to beat a hurried rhythm. He led her towards the little pavilion, its gold dome glittering in the moonlight, and in the doorway he stopped, and turned her to him, and at last, at long last, he drew his wife into his embrace, and set his mouth on hers. For the first time, now, he gave his need free rein.

After an endless time, he lifted his head. Shakira's senses

were reeling, her blood thick in her veins, like warm honey, as he led her into the pavilion.

"Oh!" she exclaimed, remembering. "Oh, this is just like my dream!"

The pavilion had been made for love. Its high arched openings gave out onto the drunken, perfumed night, over the courtyard, the playing fountains, the drooping blossom, the diamond-encrusted sky. Inside, a wide divan was strewn with pillows and cushions, and covered with lushly embroidered tapestries in a feast of the richest colours she had ever seen. Floor and walls decorated with intricate tiles from another age, and a domed ceiling where arches descended like angels, all a-glitter with mirror and gold, were lighted by the moon and stars, and by a dozen lamps, whose flames glowed inside lamps of filigree and damascene, crystal and jewel, and sculpted brass.

A low, delicately carved marble table, inlaid with leaves of ebony and chalcedony, and traced with gold, was spread with the feast that had been prepared for them. Plates of beaten gold and silver and intricately painted porcelain held a dozen different dishes, succulent and spiced, whose odours were ambrosia to their senses.

Sharif Azad al Dauleh led his wife to the divan and propped cushions under her as she sat smiling up into his eyes, her dress falling in a luxurious ripple all around her, trailing over cushions and down to the floor—a sparkling, glittering sea of green silk shot with rivulets of gold.

Leaning over her, on arms whose strength was not disguised by the fine silk of his own jacket, he bent his head to kiss and tease her lips with a taste more delicious than any food. Warmth rippled through her body, and desire flowed like honey under her skin.

He sank down onto the floor beside her, his knees folded as in the antique miniatures, the lamplight glinting on the tamed dark curls and the rich dark jewel on his hand, love shining in his eyes.

Princess Shakira lay against the cushions, also like those ancient miniature paintings, and opened her mouth to receive the succulent offerings from his fingers. Morsels of exquisitely spiced meat and vegetable, sumptuously prepared, luscious with fine oils, wrapped in delicate pastry, dipped in rich sauces, he fed her, and in between each taste his own tongue licked a last droplet from her trembling mouth.

Her heart leapt with each caress, and she knew that desire pulsed in him, too, with a need that was both pain and pleasure.

Wine he poured from a crystal decanter painted with gold, then lifted the gold-chased goblet in a strong, dark hand whose jewel flickered with molten green flame. In the lamplight the goblet, too, glowed so richly with claret and gold it hurt her.

Her senses became confused then, so that his kisses were delicious and the food a caress. A sugared strawberry kissed her lips and shivered in her blood; his tongue was spiced as it traced the curve of her lips, his mouth honey as it moved over her throat, in the curve of her arm, her palm.

Sharif's hands were music and fire as they stroked and held her through the richly embroidered silk of her dress, and she heard the music and felt the heat of the fire as if there were one sense that understood both. Sensation flicked and curled around her, as his tongue on her tongue, his fingers in her hair.

"My beloved, my wife," he murmured low, and her blood sang at the grateful triumph in his voice. "How long I have waited for you!"

She smiled, and for the first time had the confidence to tease. "Was it really so long? A few months?"

His eyes burned deep into hers. "I have waited for you, my Princess, all my life, and longer."

She gasped, for so it felt to her, too. "Yes," she whispered.

His hand moved to her throat, and she felt the tiny button at her neck submit to his fingers' firm authority. His mouth followed his hand, kissing each area of skin revealed by the parting folds of silk. The silk rustled as if it, too, trembled at the touch, and fell back willingly to expose her shoulders to him. Gently he lifted her and drew the tunic down, so that the lamplight played on the soft, smoky skin of her shoulders and arms. Now his mouth bent to the soft curve of her breast above the ruched and beaded green silk of her bodice, and she shuddered with pleasure at each kiss, each warm breath.

At last he lay down beside her, and drew her up to bend over him in the tender lamplight that burnished her curls and his. His hands stroked the skin of her shoulders, slid down over silk to her waist and hips, holding her with a firmness that thrilled her.

His eyes burned her, and his mouth smiled a smile of too much feeling.

"Shakira," he whispered. "*Allah*, how love tears the heart!" Then his hands cupped her small head, and drew her down to the hunger of his mouth.

His hands were warm on her skin, sending a potent melting into her bones, and she whimpered with need, like a small animal seeking comfort. His fingers found the hidden fastening of her bodice, and with a small noise of satisfaction he opened it.

"Oh," she cried, for everything was new, so new to her.

"There is nothing to fear," he urged softly. "You are my life, Shakira. I can never do anything to hurt you, so long as I live."

Her lips trembled into a smile. "I'm not afraid."

Now she was naked except for the silky green trousers, like a harem girl of old. Her breasts shivered alive as they pressed against the silk of his shirt, and the strong chest underneath.

His hand cupped one small, firm breast with possessive knowing, as if both hand and breast had been created only for this moment. His palm whispered back and forth, sending rumours of his intentions to her stomach and legs, down her back, along her arms, till even her fingertips understood.

Then, in sudden impatience, he leaned up to strip off his own pearl-embroidered jacket. Bare chested, wearing the white shalwar, he looked like a genie from a lamp for a moment, but then he stood to strip the shalwar down his legs, and her eyelids drooped, for he was a genie no longer, but a man.

"Oh!" she cried again.

He extinguished all lamps but one, bringing a protective blanket of dream and shadow to shroud them. He bent over her in the faint lamplight, his hand possessive under her neck and head, his mouth drinking pleasure from hers as if he were starved of it. Then he lifted his kiss and moved it to her neck, her throat, her body. Outside a night bird whistled a delicious, drunken melody in her ears like the music of his lips against her skin.

She wandered in a garden of longing as his mouth traced over her breasts, her stomach, and her hand found his head and her fingers ruffled the dark silk of his hair, twining themselves in curls. He turned his head and caught her hand, drawing it to his mouth, and sucked the palm. Pleasure shot through her with electric intensity, and she bent one knee up and hugged her thigh against his arm.

He let go her hand then, and slipped his palm down to cup the small firm mound under the green silk, watching her face for the pleasure of seeing the desire that whispered across it.

"Oh!" she cried again. "Oh, Sharif!"

She arched up into his hand, and he smiled with satisfaction, and with the strain of leashing his hungry need. As his hand caressed her, building the pleasure in her, she lifted her head and looked into his eyes. In his dark gaze she read the glow of his determination, and the frown of his love. In that moment the promised pleasure erupted under his hand, and her head fell back against the pillows, and she cried her gratitude.

"Oh, I never knew!" she said.

He smiled a tender, possessive smile. "This is only the beginning, my beloved. There is much to learn, for both of us."

For a moment she was nervous, sensing the loss of control that was to come. But this was Sharif, and in the next instant the anticipation of pleasure drowned all other feeling.

She felt his hands find the fastening in the silk that wrapped her, and he drew the whispering fabric down, his mouth kissing the skin that the departing silk revealed, stomach, abdomen, and then down the length of her leg to ankle and instep. Then he lowered his kiss to her body again.

After endless time wandering in the garden of pleasure, she felt him lift his head, and his hands lifted her back onto the divan, and then his body was above her, powerful and demanding. His hand slipped under her neck, and his kiss seized her mouth, while his other hand moved to open her body to his.

The universe waited for the stroke that was the seal of their love, the great breath caught in the moment before the whirlwind is unleashed. Then he pressed into her, with a cry that was almost a plea against pain, and she understood that for him such deep need was almost torture.

Her own pain, the pain of newness, was lost in the sweep of wild joy she felt at the deep union of their bodies and souls, so that she welcomed his body in her with a singing cry. The night bird heard, and replied, and to them both it was as if all of nature joined them at the feast. He moved in her with an urgency now that could no longer be restrained, drunk on her pleasure-song.

He pushed and thrust himself into her, searching for that one place that was his and his alone, the place where there was no more hunger, no more need, only utter peace. His throat cried out his searching need, his song joining hers in a duet against the background of nature's symphony. For a long, unmeasured time the music played, and then at last they found the clear, fine note that was nature's own, and their music arced up, exploded, and cascaded back down to earth in a dome of light.

She clung to him, and felt tears of joy and gratitude drop from her lashes and take a curving path down her cheek, for she knew that her life had been healed, and her heart could hardly contain her happiness, nor her wonder at what was possible.

Epilogue

ISLANDERS LAUNCH CLASS ACTION SUIT

The Gulf Island refugees are to launch a class action suit against Mystery Resorts, Webson Attary Pharmaceuticals and their parent corporation. The islanders, who were evicted from the islands and whose homes were destroyed by the companies, will reportedly seek compensation and punitive damages in excess of $10 billion, it was announced today.

* * * * *

Silhouette® Desire®

Get swept up in

Emilie Rose's

captivating new tale...

BREATHLESS PASSION

On sale February 2005

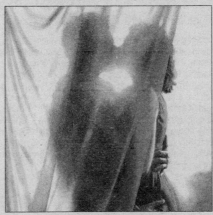

Lily West was struggling to get her business off the ground when she was offered a tantalizing proposal—pose as millionaire Rick Faulkner's fiancée and all her dreams could come true. But she was a tomboy from the wrong side of the tracks—*not* a socialite dripping charm. So Rick became Lily's tutor in the ways of sophistication...and a red-hot attraction ignited between these star-crossed lovers!

Available at your favorite retail outlet.